SAVE ME

LOGAN CHANCE

Copyright © 2017 by Logan Chance

All rights reserved. No part of this publication may be reproduced, distributed, or transmitted in any form or by any means, including photocopying, recording, or other electronic or mechanical methods, without the prior written permission of the publisher, except in the case of brief quotations embodied in critical reviews and certain other noncommercial uses permitted by copyright law.

❦ Created with Vellum

This book is dedicated to the men and women that serve our country to protect our freedom.

PROLOGUE

Answering questions. We all do it. What's your name? Where are you from?

Life is nothing but a series of questions. They start out easy in life. Two plus Two. What color is the sky?

Then, they turn harder, not as easy to answer. Where were you last night, from your parents. Why haven't you called, from a clingy girlfriend. All these questions are to learn more about you. To pry for information.

As we age, life has a way of changing these questions into something more personal, more in depth. More soul searching.

Sometimes, avoiding questions becomes a skill. Over time, people perfect the skill.

Well, I'm a fucking master. There's no one quite like me. I'm like a closed book. One that's never been read. Just sitting on the shelf, in the hopes it remains lost in the stacks of life. Because the answers to my questions are something even I can't deal with.

CHAPTER 1

CRYIN'

 Semper Fi Motherfucker

Life. Life has a funny way of turning things inside out and upside down. Joining the military was supposed to be fun, and it was at first. It was something I felt very deeply about, fighting for my country, defending our lands. College paid for? Sign me up.

But, it changed me. It took me from the boy I joined as and made me into a man. The journey wasn't always easy. It was hard as fuck, actually. There were many times during boot camp I was ready to give up. Many times, while stationed in Afghanistan I wanted to quit. But, I never did.

Of course, I never did. I didn't fight for a greater purpose. No, I fought for my fellow comrades, the men serving alongside me. My friends.

I went into the military right out of high school, wanting to live a bigger and better dream. What I got was a culture shock to my senses.

I was a boot shipped to Afghanistan right out of basic training.

And my time there is something I want to forget. Improvise, adapt and overcome. That's exactly what I did.

"Wagner, Ryan Wagner?" the nurse calls out.

I nod my head to her before rising from my seat. "That's me," I say, my 6'4 frame towering over her. She glances up from the chart she's holding and smiles.

The stark white room she leads me into makes my palms sweat. All clean and sterile. I glance at the instruments laid neatly on a silver tray and sit on the small bed, wrinkling the parchment paper.

"The doctor will be right in," the pretty blonde nurse says as she smiles to me. It's a nice smile, white teeth and full of reassurance.

The doctor enters, and spectacles and thinning hair encompass the room as his stocky frame takes a seat on the stool. His eyes are glued to my chart, and he hums softly, thumbing through the pages.

Finally, he glances up, observing the specimen sitting on the table. "Ah, Ryan. How are you today, son?"

"Great. The shoulder is still giving me problems." I'd love to tell you it happened while I was fighting off enemy intruders on our camp or during a raid in the middle of the night, but, nothing that dramatic or thrilling. I injured it during a football game between me and my men. Private Hammel tackled me, and my shoulder has never been the same.

The doctor, Dr. James, slides his glasses further up his nose as he rises to his feet. He pushes and tugs at my shoulder, and the pain is a little unbearable. Ok, more like a lot unbearable.

"I'd like for you to meet with a therapist, a physical therapist. I'll refer you," he says, making notes.

"Thanks," I say, rubbing my tender shoulder as he sets the chart down.

Dr. James grabs the light shining thing and shines it in my eyes. "Any headaches?"

"No, no headaches," I say, choking on the tongue depressor he's now trying to kill me with.

He lifts his lips, only slightly, as he checks my ears and heartbeat.

After finishing his examination, and giving me his stamp of approval, he says I'm good to go.

I hop into my red truck, remembering back to when I arrived home only a few months ago. My mother picking me up at the airport with a big smile on her face. Her eyes lighting up two shades brighter than the sun as she saw her little boy return home. I was happy to be home as well. But, when the questions overwhelmed me of my time spent overseas, I clammed up.

I didn't want to talk about my time served.

Still don't. Once I get home, my brother, Devin, knocks on my door. "Ready to go?"

"Sure, where are we going?"

He shrugs. "Out. Bar. Anywhere there's alcohol."

I laugh. "Sounds good."

Devin is not only my brother, he's one of my best friends. We're close in age, and he's always had my back.

We head out to South Beach, both of us ready to blow off steam. The bars are already packed with a good amount of people, and we decide to go into Mecca. Flashing neon lights bounce off the sweaty, gyrating bodies filling the dance floor as we weave through people on the way to the bar. My eyes roam from one hot chick to the next. A curvy brunette winks at me. Nice.

Devin smirks when he notices me eyeing up a few of the ladies and shakes his head as he orders us both a beer. Not to sound like an asshole, but he knows I'm a pussy magnet. Women love a military man. But, he's not hurting for attention. From what I hear, his band is well known in the local club scene. He's the lead vocalist for some group, Twisted Monks, he and his friends started a few years ago. I've heard a few demo cd's, but have yet to hear them perform live. That's what happens when you're gone for four years—your brother becomes a local semi-celebrity.

He hands me a beer and I glance the bar once over, and that's when I see her.

Elizabeth Packer. Lizard. I haven't seen her since I've been back. We were best friends growing up, from as long as I can remember. Since we were knee-high to a grasshopper, plucking seashells from the Miami shore. Since we both could stay the night at each other's homes with no questions asked. Of course, sleepovers stopped once puberty hit, and I was waking up with morning wood.

Lizard, Lizzy Packer, sits with a group of girls, and I take in her clingy, little black dress and heels. Her long blonde hair tumbles past her bare shoulders. She's pretty. Beautiful, actually.

"Look who's here," I say to Devin, pointing in the direction of Lizzy and her friends.

"Who's that?" His eyes flit over to her and then back to me.

"Lizzy. You remember her, right?"

He turns back around to get a better look. "Holy shit. She's hot."

"Yeah," I breathe before taking a long pull of my beer.

She's definitely changed from when we were kids.

I set my beer down, square my shoulders, and make my way over to her.

"Lizard?" I ask, stepping up close to her ear to be heard over the loud beat of the music.

She looks over at me, and her light brown eyes go wide as she smiles. "Oh, my God, Cryin'?"

Her nickname for me makes me cringe. Let me explain something before you hear it from someone else.

Third grade. A huge tree. You're invincible when you're nine. I felt I could climb to the top, maybe jump from the branches onto another neighboring tree. I was so wrong.

I'll never forget falling, nothing to break my descent but a rock...I slammed into it hard. Luckily for me, nothing broke. Kid's bodies are much more resilient to superhero actions and stupid conquests. A few tears might have been shed. Hence, the nickname Cryin' Ryan.

But, if you call me that I may have to hurt you...and not in the fun, kinky way.

"Yeah, yeah, it's me," I answer her, with the biggest shit-eating grin on my face. It feels so good to be talking to her.

CHAPTER 2

LIZARD

> " Every girl has that one guy, she has a crush on forever.

Wow, now that's a blast from the past. It's been four years since I've seen Ryan Wagner. Four years since I've heard from him at all. I forgot how tall he is. Even in my heels, I feel tiny next to him.

He looks good. Really, really good. Gone is the boy from high school and in his place, is this... military man. A very sexy military man with sculpted muscles and chiseled features. I feel like saluting him and doing anything he commands. Ok, no more cocktails for me tonight.

Lexi elbows me as I gawk, and I clear my throat to introduce Ryan and his younger brother, Devin, to my best friends Lexi and Belinda.

"Hey, I've heard you sing," Lexi says, pointing at Devin. "Remember," she says to Belinda, "we went out after the Heat game."

"Ah, Heat fans?" Devin asks, and before you know it, the three of them are lost in a basketball conversation.

"How have you been?" Ryan asks, smiling the boyish grin that used to get him into trouble in high school. It got him out of trouble many times, too. It's its very own lethal weapon.

"I've been great. How was the war?" I slur the words, and someone should really take my drink away from me.

Ryan cracks a smile. "Well, I survived. So, I guess that's a win."

"I'm glad you're here." I lean into hug him, and Ryan's strong arms wrap around my body, lifting me off the ground. I want to live in this moment. Not wanting him to put me down ever. He smells delicious.

The moment my feet hit the floor, the spell is broken. This is Ryan. I'm not going to act like some school-aged groupie.

No, I did enough of that in high school. So, I reposition my skirt and return my senses back to the friend I have always been to him.

But, fuck he's gorgeous. And, I know Belinda agrees. She stares at him like he's the next new item on the value menu at McDonald's.

I'll let you in on a little secret, if you haven't guessed already—I had a major crush on Ryan in high school. He never felt the same, and I never pursued anything, but the minute he wrapped his arms around me, and the smell of his cologne wafted over me, it took me right back there. Sixteen and starry eyed. Seriously, someone cut me off.

I push my Margarita away from me and gaze back into his light green eyes as he leans in closer. "How many of these have you had?" He motions to my sour cocktail, and I smile.

"That obvious?"

"It's cute." He winks. "Last time I saw you drunk was at Julie's graduation party."

Oh god, you know how you have a moment you wish you could take back? That was mine. I was drunk. All the big mistakes start with those three words, don't they? Anyway, he was leaving for the military, and, well, I was feeling sentimental. Liquid courage led me to kiss him that night. There was no tongue involved, just a lingering kiss on his full lips. But, a week later he shipped off to boot camp, and that's all she wrote. Not that he took it seriously or anything. I shake my head. "Don't remind me. That was a bad night."

He shrugs. "Not too bad."

My cheeks heat. "Yeah, right." I slap his arm. "I promise we won't be having a repeat of that night."

"Oh, that's too bad." My eyes widen. Is he serious? He gazes at my lips for a second too long and it warms my skin.

I lean in, contemplating replaying the kiss I planted on Ryan at Julie's graduation party, but before I can make a fool of myself for a second time, a familiar voice interrupts, "Ryan Wagner?"

I'd know that voice anywhere. It taunted me many times in high school. Ryan's ex-girlfriend, Anna Scott. Maybe girlfriend is too strong. They dated a week before Ryan cut her loose. Casually, I straighten my posture and smile at the girl who hated me for no other reason than I was Ryan's best friend. Lots of girls did. It wasn't easy being his friend, but I stuck it out.

She gives me a tight smile, and then steps closer to Ryan. "What are you doing here?"

He looks down at her and then steps closer to me. "I'm catching up with Lizzy."

She looks between us and then barely hides the disdain in her blue eyes. "Well it was good running into you, Ryan," she says, taking her drink from the bartender. "See you around."

"Not if I see you first," I mumble.

Ryan laughs. "She didn't seem very happy to see you."

"Well, I'm the devil, remember?"

He laughs again, stepping even closer. There is no space left between us. "Yeah, well, where are you hiding the horns in that get up?" Am I imagining we're having a moment? I really wish I hadn't had that third margarita. His eyes drift down my body as he takes a long pull of his beer.

Devin, Lexi, and Belinda have all abandoned us for the dance floor, and it's suddenly hot in here. Mainly because, here's Ryan looking sexy as hell, and Connor and his friend, Erik, Lexi's brother, are coming this way.

Shit.

I've been on one date with Connor. Maybe there's a second date on the horizon, but it's not something I want to think about right now. I plaster on a fake smile as they walk over. Kayla, Erik's girlfriend, waves to me.

"Hey, Lizzy," Connor says, walking up to Ryan and I, placing his arm around me. He's posturing, and it's uncomfortable and my eyes immediately seek Ryan's out. He doesn't seem to mind, so I pretend I don't either.

After I introduce everyone, and explain how Ryan is an old friend from school,

Ryan and Devin end up leaving, and I'm left alone with Connor. But, my mind is all occupied with Ryan Wagner.

∼

CHAPTER 3

CRYIN'

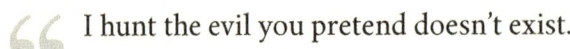 I hunt the evil you pretend doesn't exist.

Who the fuck was that asshole? Sure, running into Lizzy was great, until that redheaded jerk walked up and put his arm around her.

Wonder how serious things are with them? Ah, fuck. Who am I to care about any of that. She's a friend, or she used to be. So, who cares if she's dating that guy? Lizzy had a few guys she dated in high school, and I never thought twice about it. Unless they were assholes, then I made it my business.

Devin and I continue walking down South Beach, and I shrug off the thoughts of Lizzy.

"Glad you came out?" Devin asks.

"Yeah." And I am. This is the first time we've hung out together since I've been home.

"Lizzy's hot. You get her number?" he asks as we head into a low-key bar.

"Nah. She's with that other guy."

"That loser? I think you should give her a call. You could use a piece of ass," he says.

I flinch when he speaks of Lizzy that way. She was always just a friend. "Yeah, maybe." I change the subject as we check out the newest hotspot in Miami.

Later that night, when I'm damn near falling asleep, Lizzy's bright smile enters my mind, and I fall asleep wondering what if.

A few days later, I walk up the steps to the physical therapist's office. It's hot, like always in Florida, and my shoulder and neck throb. I step into the large waiting area. Elevator music plays from overhead, and the soft murmurs of patients in the chairs along the wall fill my ears as I step up to the nurse's desk to sign in. Well hell. I glance up and none other than Lizzy stands by the reception desk, concentrating on a chart in front of her. Guess Lizzy made her dream of being a physical therapist a reality. I feel like an ass for not knowing. Her wavy blonde hair and pink scrubs are a patient's wet dream. When did she get such perfect tits? And a curvy ass that makes me wonder what kind of panties she's wearing? The high ponytail on her head reminds me of all the times we were little and would hang out at the roller rink. She has on these dangly surfboard earrings that make me smile. She looks up, sees me, and waves her hand. "Ryan, hey."

Smiling, I wave back before taking a seat.

Half an hour later, she comes into the waiting area and calls my name.

I follow her through two sets of doors, and as she leads me into a tiny room, my breath catches.

I don't know what I was thinking earlier, but I sure as fuck didn't expect me and her in a private room together. I step past the threshold while she acts like nothing phases her.

Of course it doesn't. I'm overreacting. This is her job. She's a professional. I move inside the dimly lit room and she turns to me. "Ok, I need you to remove your shirt and lie down on the table."

By table...she means bed. It's a full on bed. Well, more so than the normal doctor's exam table.

With one hand, I tug at the back of the neckline and pull the material over my head. Her eyes drift up from the chart and skim over my chest, down to my abs, and back up.

"Nice tattoo," she says, referring to the eagle inked over my heart.

Tossing the t-shirt on a chair along the wall, I turn around to get on the 'table' and shift trying to get comfortable. "Thanks."

"I need you on your stomach," she says, with a low sultriness I never noticed before in her voice.

"Oh, sorry." I flip over to my stomach and try to relax.

"Today, I'm just going to start with a deep tissue massage of your neck, shoulders, and back. Just relax and enjoy."

She presses play on some light music, and I close my eyes. Her lotioned-hands make contact with my skin, and my heart tumbles into a lost abyss inside my soul. Her hands are magical, kneading into my muscles with the perfect amount of pressure. She was made for this.

The song whispers memories of dancing with a lost love, and I relax. My eyes stay shut through the whole massage, but my heart beats a slow steady rhythm.

My mind drifts back to our senior year, just at the last hour of prom. I went with some girl...Heather, or maybe Holly. Either way, I was having a horrible time. Lizzy showed up with some jackass from band. I think he played the trombone or something.

I already knew I'd be signing up for the military right after graduation, and Lizzy wasn't happy about me going away.

She found me outside, while I waited for my date to say goodbye to everyone in the school. I leaned against my father's

Ford Taurus, checking the doors every time they opened, hoping my date would finally be ready to go to the after party we were invited to.

The doors opened, only it wasn't Heather, it was her...Lizard.

I laughed as she made her way toward me. "Where's Mr. Seventy-Six Trombones?"

She smiled. "Oh, you know, he's off leading the big parade somewhere."

She moved closer, inching her hand closer to my chest. "Ryan," she whispered.

"Yeah, what's wrong?"

Her hand landed on my chest, and I glanced down to gaze into her soft brown eyes. "Promise me you won't lose contact with me when you leave. Promise me you'll stay safe and come home." Tears welled in her eyes, and I wiped a stray water droplet as it raced down her cheek.

"Lizard, I promise. You're my best friend. It's me and you forever."

Only problem is, I didn't keep my promise to her. I never wrote her, called her...nothing. I've been back for three months and never looked her up. I wanted to, but sometimes life gets in the way.

My body warms as her hands roam over my skin, and all the blood rushes to my cock. Fuck. Hard is not what I want to be right now, but her hands are creating the perfect amount of friction, and, well, it's turning me on. She slides her hands over my shoulders and a moan escapes. Shit.

I shouldn't be reacting this way. Her hands pause for the briefest of seconds before she continues working my muscles into oblivion and sighs. "You never even wrote to me, Ryan," she says over the soft music.

I lift my head from the oval cutout where it was wedged. "What?" I sit up, without thinking, gazing up at her.

"You promised you wouldn't lose touch, but you did."

I will my hard on to go away, and grab both her hands, rubbing my thumbs across her soft skin. "Lizzy, I'm so so so sorry. It was hell over there. I was in a strange mindset. And, well, I wanted to write you many times. But, one week turned into two, and after a while, I didn't know what to say."

She slaps my good shoulder, wiping a tear threatening to fall. "I missed you. Now lie back down."

"I missed you, too."

I lie back down, thanking God, she didn't notice my hard dick.

"I want us to be friends again," she says. You were always the one person I could always count on, Ryan."

Any thoughts of ever getting Lizzy naked, screaming my name, die right here in the office. Because I want to be the friend she can count on again. "I want that too." I smile, and resist the urge to take her in my arms once again.

She pushes me back down on the table and finishes off my massage with no happy ending. After my appointment, I make plans to hang out with her later to catch up over dinner and a movie.

∼

CHAPTER 4

LIZARD

　Once best friends, now strangers with memories.

His dick is huge. It's not unusual for patients to get lost in the sensations of a massage. It's happened plenty, but it took everything in me to remain professional and not gawk. It was a miracle I kept my eyes trained on his. "Hey, Lex, you home?" I call out, hanging my purse on the hook by the door.

She raises her hand from the couch, and I flick on the overhead light in the living room. "Over here," she says.

"What are you doing sitting in the dark?" I ask as I plop onto the sofa beside her.

"Thinking."

Oh no, when Lexi gets in her "thinking" moods, I usually find any reason to hightail it right out of the house we share.

"About?"

"Wondering what my purpose is. Ever since Jared and I broke

up last year, I'm just wondering if I'll ever have sex again. It's been quite a while."

I wrap an arm around her tanned shoulders. "Aw, you'll meet someone."

Exhausted from my day, I prop my feet up on the coffee table and lean back into the sofa, closing my eyes.

"Well, I hope so. I think I'm dead down there." She laughs.

"Oh gross. You're crazy."

"I'm serious. I need like a necromancer to come and resurrect my vagina back from the dead," she says, laughing.

"Stop." I swat at her.

"Call Anita Blake. I need some action."

"Who's Anita Blake?" I ask, leaning up to glimpse at her.

"The vampire hunter. She brings things back from the dead."

"Stop. You'll meet someone. It's been a long time for me too. Maybe I should call Anita." It has been a while since I've had sex, and all my thoughts turn to Ryan. I shouldn't even go there.

"I was also thinking about that gorgeous guy, Ryan, from the club. Was that his name? What about hooking me up?"

I bolt upright. Did she just read my mind? "My Ryan? Uh, I mean, um, maybe. I don't think he'd be a good fit for you."

What's wrong with me? I should jump at the chance to hook Ryan and Lexi up. They're both great. But, my heart beats double time at the thought. Is it hot in here?

"Oh, ok. Well, Kayla is trying to get me to use the dating app I used for my brother, Erik. It's how they met, remember?"

I lean back, glad the attention is off Ryan and back onto something else. Something safe. I nod as she tells me the story of Kayla and Erik meeting again. I've heard the story a few times before and always laugh along as she describes the big mix-up between them.

"Oh, by the way, how's Connor? What happened the other night after the club?"

"Uh, nothing. He's nice, but I don't think I'm that into him."

And, I don't think I am. From the moment Ryan walked over at the club, I haven't been able to stop thinking about him. His eyes. His smile. His muscles.

Ryan has everything going for him in the looks department, and I know he has a personality to match. He has a boyish way about him—a shyness I find fascinating.

He's perfect, really. But, I can't think of that. I would never want to harm our friendship. A friendship we both took a lifetime to build. One that I'll cherish forever. So, as delectable as he may be...he's still just Cryin' Ryan, and I'd never cross that line with him.

"What are you doing tonight?" Lexi asks, pulling me back to the present.

"Huh? Oh, I'm hanging out with Ryan tonight. We're going to have dinner and maybe catch a movie." I rise from the couch. "I better get ready."

Lexi's eyes examine me, surveying my features, and I try my best to hide any desire for my friend from her prying eyes.

"Sure. Well, you kids have fun." She closes her eyes. "I'll be here wallowing in self pity."

I push on her legs, laughing. "Oh give me a break. You should call up Belinda and go out."

"Maybe," she answers as I trod off to my bedroom to get ready for my date with Ryan. I mean meet-up. This is not a date. Even if part of me kind of wishes it were.

Two hours later, I'm nestled in the passenger side of Ryan's red pickup truck. The truck he's had since high school.

"I've missed this truck," I say as he turns down the street leading out to South Beach.

"Me too. Much better than the Humvees I'm used to always being in."

"Oh, what was that like?"

He smiles, his eyes meeting mine for a split second before resting back on the road. "The Humvees? They broke down a lot. Not like my baby here." He laughs, patting the dashboard with his hand.

I laugh along with him as we pull up to a poppin' little bistro in the heart of the city.

"What's up with Big Red?" he asks after we've been seated and gotten our drinks from the server.

My brows pull together in confusion. "Who?"

"That guy from the club the other night."

"Well, nothing, really." Ryan's hazy eyes land on my mouth as I speak. "We've been on like one date."

His eyes drift back to mine and he nods. The server grabs our attention, going over the specials for the evening and Ryan grins.

"We'll have two cheeseburgers," he glances at me, "You still like burgers, right?" I nod. "Two cheeseburgers, one no pickle or tomato, and fries." He snaps his menu shut with affirmation and my heart skips a little beat that he remembers how I like mine. The waitress beams at him before leaving us.

"You look different," he whispers, leaning in, his arms resting on the table.

I smile, praying it's a compliment. "So do you." This is my Ryan, but altered. His light brown hair that always turned golden in the Miami sun is short, buzzed closely, from the military. His familiar light moss-green eyes look more world weary, and the way they rake over my body have me suddenly feeling underdressed. Naked, actually.

"God, this is so awkward. It feels like I don't even know you anymore."

The waitress returns, sliding a basket of bread on the table. I've been to this restaurant many times and you do *not* get a basket of bread. My eyes narrow at the fluffy rolls and then at the wide grin she gives Ryan. He thanks her, cooly, like he was born with charm and charisma. Gone is the awkward kid I once knew. In his place, this man. This man whose biceps are as big as my head. Ok, not literally, but hmm, maybe they are. I can't peel my eyes away from him.

Finally, I answer, "I'm still the same me." And, I am. Nothing has changed. Not even this crush I have, apparently. Had. The crush I had.

"Ever take your telescope out anymore?"

"I haven't in a long time." I'm an astrology nerd. There, I've said it.

"Did you ever find it?"

"It?"

"The Cryin' Lizard?" He smiles.

"Oh, I forgot about that star."

"Well, thanks."

I lean over, grabbing his hand. "No no no. Not like that. It was the best present anyone has ever given me."

You guessed it. Ryan bought me a star for my sweet sixteen birthday. He named it after our nicknames. And, the Cryin' Lizard is so well hidden in the night sky, I don't think I'll ever find it. "No, I've given up hope. Maybe one day."

"Don't give up. Remember what I told you? When you least expect it, you'll find it staring back at you."

"Yeah, I remember." I smile, grabbing a roll. No need for the basket of flirt to go to waste.

"You would have loved Afghanistan." I raise my eyebrows. "Well, ok, not loved. But, the stars were always out and perfect. No city lights to drown them out."

"How was it over there?"

He leans back, crossing his arms across his broad chest. He changes the subject without answering, "So, how's Alice?"

Unsure of why he doesn't want to answer and not wanting to push the subject, my mood deflates. He's had a crush on my older sister, Alice, since junior high school. I'm half excited to tell him Alice is married, but at the same time, a little sad that he may still be harboring feelings for her, and I'm about to crush his heart. I rip the band-aid. "She's married."

He doesn't answer, simply takes another sip of his wine and offers a tight-lipped smile.

Finally, he speaks, softly, "Oh, that's good."

Something is off with him now. I'm not sure if it was the mention of his time overseas or the Alice news. Whatever it is, I feel an overwhelming need to fix it. "Old crushes die hard, huh?" I should know.

He shakes his head and sits up straighter. "No, no. It wasn't really a crush at all. Sorry, I just don't like talking about my time overseas." He smiles, and I drop the subject as he glances around the restaurant. He nods his head, in the direction of an elderly couple. "What do you think their story is?" This is a game Ryan and I always played.

I swivel in my chair to gain a better look. "High school sweethearts, married young. Kids...the whole nine yards," I say as I turn back around to face him.

He runs his hand down his face, contemplating their life story...or what he believes to be their story. "I think he was an international spy. They spent many years apart and have only recently connected. I mean look at them, Lizard," he points in their direction, "they're so happy to have been married for that many years."

There it is. The nickname he's called me since we were kids. The nail in the coffin of any fantasy I may have ever had of him liking me. I peek over my shoulder again, taking in the couple enjoying each other's company. The older man kisses his wife's hand. They're happy. "I don't know. Wouldn't it be great, though, to have that with someone? Someone you never tire of?"

The waitress interrupts with our burgers, and after doing everything but offering to feed him, she leaves. He ponders my statement. "Yeah, I guess. What about you? Have you dated anyone seriously since I've been gone?"

I take a deep breath and wonder how much I should tell him. He probably doesn't want to hear about Daniel, the loser from school, who I thought was 'the one' for a whole five minutes. Apparently, I was number three for him. He cheated on me with not one, but two other girls. Asshole.

Other than Daniel, there hasn't been anything too serious.

"Nothing substantial," I answer.

He beams bright, and it creates a warm feeling deep within.

We steer the rest of the conversation onto neutral topics, catching each other up on the last four years of our lives. He doesn't delve into the military talk much, but he does tell me about boot camp and the torture he went through during his time there.

I tell him about school and how I graduated top of my class. We laugh over old memories, and after dinner we decide to stroll along the path down by the beach.

CHAPTER 5

CRYIN'

> Life is ten percent what happLife is ten percent what happens to you, and ninety percent how you respond to it.ens to you, and ninety percent how you respond to it.

"Did you want to catch a movie?"

The light of the moon dances along the ocean. A soft breeze plays in her wild hair, and I turn my head to let the wind graze my face.

"I'm happy just being here," she says.

I stick my hands in the pockets of my jeans as we walk side-by-side. Many times as teenagers we'd walk this same path.

Four years is a long time to be gone. So much has changed while I was away, the city of Miami, the shops along the shore, the local movie theatre, restaurants. And Lizzy.

She holds the confidence of a gorgeous woman. It's almost intimidating. She's accomplished so much, and what have I done?

Sure, I fought for our country. Sure, I got a Purple Heart. But, sometimes I still feel like things over there were easier.

Being here, working for my father, I feel like I'm stuck in a perpetual rat race. And, I haven't even started school. Which what's the point?

At twenty-two, Lizzy is definitely beating me in the game of life.

We walk in silence a few blocks, and it isn't awkward or weird. It's one of the things I really like about her. She knows when to keep her mouth shut and not ask the questions I don't want to answer.

She glances out to the crashing waves, just off the coast. I follow her line of sight, feeling the pull of the ocean call to me.

"You ever go out anymore?" I ask her.

She crosses her arms back and forth in the air, signaling no. "Never ever again. I could never learn it good enough."

"Oh, come on. I used to teach you to surf every day during the summer."

"And if you remember I was never very good at it." She pinches my arm, and I crack a smile.

She's right. She was never very good at surfing. "Well promise me you'll let me give you another lesson."

"Are you working at your dad's surf shop still?"

I nod my head, taking one last scan of the surf. Our eyes lock, and she smiles. I feel it in my chest. It's such a pretty sight.

"Yeah," I answer.

She sighs. "I guess you should take me home. I have to be up early for work tomorrow."

I smile as I turn toward the parking lot down the street. "As you wish."

She wraps her arm into mine, and we walk back together.

When I pull into the driveway of her little cottage home, I shut off the engine, not ready to end the night. "Let me see your house."

"Ok, come on in." She hops down from the truck, and I follow her up to the blue, front door. When I step inside the tiny foyer and browse around, one word to describe it...eclectic.

Strange and unique in its own special way.

It's a hodge podge of vibrant furniture: bright red couch, some kind of weird yellow chair that looks like a half bed, and a battered trunk for a coffee table. A mural of photographs fill the charcoal grey wall in front of me, creating the constellations in the night sky. Why am I suddenly finding her nerdy love of the sky so damn sexy? It makes me want to throw her down on the thick, white rug covering the hardwood floors and fuck her while she screams out the names of them.

Instead, I revert to the familiar and tease her, "Lizard, aw, look at you all grown up." I noogie her head as she swats my hand away.

"Shut up," she jokes.

The brunette from Mecca sits on the couch. A low whistle comes from her mouth as she rises. "Well, hello, sailor." She fans herself, and I let out a soft chuckle.

"Hey. Lexi, right?" I reach my hand out to shake hers.

"Yes. It's great running into you again. Can I ask you something?"

I cringe inwardly, wondering what on earth she'll ask. "Sure, anything."

"Did you just call her Lizard?"

Lizzy steps in, pushing Lexi toward the hallway. "Ok, time for bed. Ryan, there's no need to answer her."

They exchange a glance, and I laugh. "It's a great story. One I can't believe Lizard here hasn't told you," I say as I sit down on the couch.

Lexi sidesteps Lizzy and plops down next to me. "Oh this I gotta hear."

Lizzy covers her face and slides onto the bedchair on the opposite side of the room.

"When we were kids," I start, smiling over at Lizzy, "we used to go to the community pool during the summers. Our parents would drop all us kids off. Me, my two younger brothers, Lizzy, and her sister, Alice," I hesitate at the memories of those fun times. They were innocent, we were innocent, and it sucks how life takes that away replacing it with things that change who you are.

"Please don't tell me she would eat lizards," Lexi says in disgust.

"No, I'm sure that was you," Lizzy says, laughing.

"A girl's gotta eat." Lexi laughs.

I shake my head, holding in my laughter over their repertoire. "Anyway, the concrete around the pool used to be scorching hot. And Lizzy here, would hop from foot to foot. Just like a lizard does to cool their feet. She was cute, standing on one foot, until she couldn't take it anymore, and then bouncing to the other."

"That's kind of sweet. Ever heard of flip flops?" Lexi asks, smiling at Lizzy.

"Yes, duh. But, we were young."

That's always an answer to all stupidity in your younger years. I remember back to all the years Lizzy and I got into our fair share of stupidity.

"I guess I should get going," I say, rising from the couch.

"I'll walk you out." Lizzy jumps to her feet, and her body moves toward me. Sexy as fuck. I shake my head as sexual thoughts enter my brain.

We move to the door in unison. A heavy fog clouds my vision as I only see her. Nothing else matters as I zero in on her lips. Lips I want so badly to claim. Every nerve ending in my body brings me one step closer. This is the start of my greatest fear. A fear of lusting after her. A friend.

Even though she's nothing like the friend I remember. When we were younger I never thought of her this way.

I would never clam up with the desire to touch her. But her

wild hair is begging, no pleading, with me to run my fingers through it.

Funny thing is, when we were kids, I'd touch her all the time. Many nights we'd lay awake in my small, twin bed watching TV, and she'd be nestled in my side as I ran my fingers through her hair. And not once, not once, would I ever think of her in a sexual capacity. Even when I was a teenager and my hormones were a fucking train wreck, I'd never go there with her.

But now, here, it's all I can think about. My brain is misfiring all the wrong signals to my cock, making it harden as thoughts of us nestled on my old twin bed play through my memory. Her long legs, round ass, and perky tits tease me underneath her outfit, and I swallow hard as she opens the door for me.

She's the same as always around me, so obviously I'm the only one with these thoughts. If she had any want or need for me, she'd be feeling the same things as me. She wouldn't be acting like I'm a neutral party standing here.

But, she is. She's treating me the same as her best friend in there on the couch. So, I hug her goodnight and walk away to my truck.

∽

The next morning, I enter my father's surf shop to get ready for a long day at work. Let me tell you about my dad.

He's your typical beach bum, only he's not a bum at all. His surf shop is one of the hottest spots in South Beach.

Sure, it's no Ron Jon's...but his little shop gets some serious action. I like to think of it like this—Ron Jon's is for the tourists, while Funk You Boards is for all the locals.

My father is a great man. Been surfing his whole life. Taught me to surf at the ripe ol' age of five. His unfulfilled dreams of going pro were passed on to me and my younger brothers. Out of the three of us, only my youngest brother, Lance, is living the dream. Still in high school and competing against champions. Yep, you heard that right...I'm related to a pro surfer. Which doesn't really get me very far, but in the surfing community it sure does.

Everyone knows who we are. The Wagner's. The surf experts.

My father spots me near the register and walks over. "Hey, son," he says, sounding high as fuck. But, he isn't. He's never even touched the stuff, or so he claims. But, I'm sure back in the seventies he was all over that shit. He runs a hand through his shoulder length, sun bleached, blond hair and smiles.

Yeah, this is daddy dearest. You think my dad is a character, wait until you meet my mom. And just on cue, she comes out of the back room. "Ryan?" She rushes over, like she didn't just see me yesterday, hugging me and pampering me with kisses. I'm twenty-two, not twelve, but she doesn't care. She's a complete beach bimbette. Well, I know that sounds mean...but just wait.

"Did you do the inventory for last night, Barb?" my father asks her.

My mother purses her lips, flipping her blonde hair over her shoulder as her blue eyes wander toward the ceiling, hoping the answers she needs are there.

She's like an older Pamela Anderson without the huge rack. My mother never got on the fake boob train like most Miamians. Or the fake lips, either. Ok, my mother has nothing fake except the blonde color of her hair. And, for an older woman, she's kinda hot. Sure, she's my mom...but, I know other guys think she's a full on milf.

"I think I did," she finally answers. "I'm not really sure, Loren."

My father smiles, kissing her on the top of her head. "It's ok, dear. We'll just have Ryan do it."

I roll my eyes. "Thanks." I grab the clipboard from behind the shelf and head toward the back-storage room.

I count the boards two at a time letting my thoughts wander to Lizzy. The fact she's back in my life has me smiling all day, until I need to leave for my weekly appointment with Dr. James.

The doctor's office is the last place I want to be. There isn't a single cloud in the sky, and it's perfect weather to grab my board and hit the beach. I fire off a text to Lizzy, asking her to join me after my appointment.

She agrees, and it makes my smile wider as I enter Dr. James's office. He goes over my vitals asking the normal questions. Headaches? No. Nausea? No. Muscle aches? No.

All is good, and I head back to my little bungalow...ok, yes, it's on my parent's property. But, it's still mine. I know you all were wondering how I afford anything...well, I get by.

I grab my board, and a board for Lizard, and head off to the beach.

Spotting Lizzy's little Vespa, I pull into the spot right next to it.

Her blonde hair is wild when I step onto the beach. The sand is hot beneath my feet, and I rush off to where she sits on a towel waiting for me.

"Ready to do this, Mrs. Davenport?"

She shields her eyes as she tilts her head to gander up at me. "Oh, why Mr. Davenport, I thought you'd never show," she says in the most twangiest of southern accents. My heart beats a little faster that she remembers the silly names we called each other.

She outstretches her hand, and I haul her body from her spot. She giggles, and we head off toward the deep blue.

Don't think I didn't notice the skimpy getup she's barely wearing. Because believe me, it's all I can stare at. I can't turn away. That's why I grabbed her so quick. An urge to throw a towel over her, to keep anyone from looking at the full breasts exposed by the tiny top, nearly overwhelms me. The only thing stopping me is the fact I wouldn't be able to see them if I did. Fuck. Maybe this wasn't such a great idea.

∼

CHAPTER 6

LIZARD

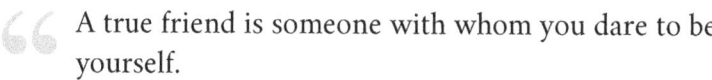 A true friend is someone with whom you dare to be yourself.

The way he's focused on me sends goosebumps igniting across my skin. The beach is packed with tourists and locals, everyone searching for the perfect spot along the shore, but it feels as if we're alone.

"Just watch me for a few waves, then we'll get you started. Do you remember everything I taught you ages ago?"

"I...uh, no. Not really," I confess.

His smile is engaging, and I listen to his instructions as the seagulls squawk high in the sky.

The heated sun on my skin mixed with the smell of coconut from my tanning lotion, makes me remember how much I used to love coming here with him.

The white crest of the waves crash around his knees as he moves further out into the ocean. I worry momentarily about his shoulder, but it's not really that bad of an injury. He should be fine.

The cool waves break at my feet as I stand in awe studying him. His smile is contagious as he focuses on the upcoming wave in the distance. He's always loved surfing, and I always loved watching him.

When he mentioned joining the military, my heart cracked. I'll never tell him how I would visit the beach after he left, listening to the waves crash as I thought about him on the other side of the world. Praying he was safe, melancholy because I hadn't heard from him. Those are things he doesn't need to know.

I can't help but smile as Ryan lies along his board, paddling toward the shore. The wave picks him up, and he hops to his feet.

God, his chest should be illegal. So sculpted and chiseled. Planes and ripples everywhere. Grooves I'd like to explore with my tongue.

I snap to attention, mesmerized, as he rides the wave out, his board moving under his direction. His body dips and turns, and he makes it look so easy. It's not easy at all for me, though.

Shit. I'm going to have to do that soon, because here he comes. His dripping wet body walks up to me.

"You ready, sunshine?"

Unsure, I scowl, furrowed brows and narrowed eyes trained on him. "I guess."

"Let me show you a few basics," he says, bending over to position my board on the wet sand. "Step on," he urges.

When my feet are planted on the board, the feel of his hands on my waist startles me. Chills race all over, hardening my nipples.

"You want to be centered on the board." He squats, and his hand nudges my legs apart. His head is eye level with my pussy, and, suddenly, this skimpy, pink bikini doesn't seem like such a great idea. "Open your legs for me," he says, and maybe it's my imagination, but his voice just dropped an octave.

"Ok." I inch my feet up on the board. No lie, his face is nearly between my legs. His dog tags catch the sunlight against his bare chest, and I can't speak. His soft touch, roaming down my legs, ignites something in me, making me wet before I ever get in the ocean.

He runs his hand down my back, stopping just above my bikini bottom. If you can call it that. It barely covers my ass. "Lie on the board."

I do as he says, and I swear I hear him curse under his breath. My bikini rides up, and I reposition it as his eyes glaze over, eyeing me closely.

"Ok," seems to be the only word I can utter.

"You'll want to paddle as fast as you can when the wave comes." His hands glide up my sides, to my shoulders, and now I'm really getting turned on. My hard nipples press into the board beneath me, probably carving out a new logo, as I squirm under his "basics" training. His touch borders on sensual. Does he realize this? How am I supposed to pay attention? My thighs squeeze together when his fingers trace under the thin strap of my suit.

I glimpse over my shoulder and his gaze narrows on me, his hand not stopping its trek along my heated skin. He licks his lips, and I need to cool off.

"I'm ready," I lie.

He stares at me a beat before nodding and helping me up. His eyes drift down to my nipples covered by the two teeny triangles, and he scrubs his hand across his jaw. "Let's do it," he says. Oh, I want to do it alright.

We paddle our boards out together and sit, straddling them, with our feet dangling in the water. "This is nice," I say.

"I love surfing. I've missed it so much while being trapped in that sandbox overseas."

My eyes scan along the coast, perusing the many families enjoying the afternoon weather. "Was it really bad?"

"Not always."

We bob along, not really paying attention to the waves anymore.

I debate on asking more. Chewing my bottom lip, I decide to question further. "What were some of the good things?" I smile and peer at him.

The sun reflects off his brown hair, casting it into an almost golden color. Light reflects in each water droplet trickling down his tanned chest. "The guys I served with," he answers. "They were some of the greatest men I've ever known."

I run my fingers along my board. "Do you still keep in touch?"

"Yeah, sometimes." He glances over his shoulder, spotting the perfect wave. Excitement lights his eyes. "Let's try for this one."

We both lie flat on our boards and paddle. Ryan is a pro, he catches the wave with ease and hops to his feet.

Me, not so much. The wave picks me up, but I'm not quick enough on the jump. The wave passes me, and Ryan rides the swell out.

When he spots me on my board, I raise my hand. "I don't know what happened, man. I tried," I call out.

He laughs, slightly, as he paddles back to where I am. He pushes at my shoulder, almost causing me to go down. "Hey," I say.

"Did you not do like I showed you?"

I roll my eyes. "Easier said than done, hotshot."

"Let's try again."

We keep trying for another hour until I finally declare I'm unteachable. Hey, it's not my fault. Some people just can't be taught certain things. I'm ok with it.

After, we hit an ice cream shop with exotic flavors and a 1950's vibe with red, leather padded barstools and a mammoth red and gold jukebox in the corner.

This was quite the hotspot back in the day. I spot the pinball machine. "Care to make a wager?" I ask Ryan, pointing in the direction of the antique squared away between a small dinette set and an old-school soda fountain.

He looks at the machine and back at me. "You're on. What's the bet?"

I purse my lips, tapping my chin. "If I lose, I'll...um, clean your house for a week?"

"In a french maid costume?" His tone is serious, and it sends chills over my skin. I stare at him, until he can no longer keep up the facade and cracks a smile. "How about if I win, I get to decide where we go this weekend?" he asks.

"And if I win, I'll pick the activity," I agree, my heart warming to the thought he wants to hang out with me.

We walk over, slide quarters in the machine, and Ryan fires away. He's good. I'll give him that. He slams into the machine with his hips, and then my face grows hot. He is fucking this machine, gripping the sides as if it's a woman's body. He pounds again, and my thoughts fall further into the gutter. A picture of him thrusting into me invades my mind, and I push it away as best I can. It's not easy pretending not to notice how his muscles flex and work the machine like he owns it. Nothing else exists except the tension in his face as he focuses on the task at hand. His teeth capture his bottom lip as he concentrates. The machine should be put away after his abuse on it. Retired to a dusty abandoned warehouse, never to be played again.

He finishes his round, smiling at his 300 score. When he turns around, we're close. Too close. My body warms, a burn that explodes in my chest and travels out through my skin.

"Do you think you can beat me, little girl?" he asks looking down at me. The challenge in his voice sends a shiver through my body.

I swallow. "I feel like I need a cigarette after watching that, but I think I can handle it," I reply, faking a confidence I no longer have.

"Let's see what ya got." For the next minute or so, my

concentration is solely on the game. Yeah, on the game. I don't notice him inching closer behind me. Or the way his ocean scent wreaks havoc on my senses. I try to pretend I can't feel his chest pressed lightly against my back. I lean forward a bit, causing my ass to brush against his groin. Oh, God. Concentrate.

His lips brush my ear. "I wonder what else you can handle," he whispers.

My ball completely sinks, and I lose the round. The hairs on the nape of my neck rise, and I close my eyes a beat too long when his hand slides onto the small of my back.

Swirling around, I push against his chest. "Cheater," I whisper.

Heated eyes, heavy breathing, and a complete want thickens the stuffy air of the shop.

"All's fair at the ice cream shop." His husky tone hardens my nipples.

"Is it?" His eyes drop to my mouth. The jingle of the door when a customer enters jolts me from my haze.

Ryan doesn't appear fazed in the least.

"It is." He leans in, and I close my eyes, waiting, hoping, for the kiss I pray he lays on me.

Before anything happens, someone comes up behind him, calling his name.

"Been a long time, man. How the hell are ya?" Timothy Rivers comes into my vision.

Ryan is on point, shaking his hand, pretending that 'almost kiss' didn't just take place.

"Hey Lizzy, how are you? Figures you two would be here together. Always joined at the hip," Timothy's nasally voice says.

Timothy still lives at home, and I'm pretty sure his mother still does his laundry among other things. Never had a girlfriend that I can remember, because he's rude. He used to tease me mercilessly when I had braces. Timothy isn't all bad, but the moment they start talking about sports, I bail.

I head off down the path to the boardwalk, one of my favorite places.

It isn't a boardwalk like Atlantic City or Daytona, just some slabs of wood that stretch out over the ocean. I take a stroll, passing by older men with their buckets of caught fish and poles in their retired hands.

Waves crash against the shore, and the salty air, coated with a hint of bait and tackle, fills my lungs. I love the smell of summer. My mind drifts back to the almost kiss, and as if I conjured him up, his voice startles me, "Lizzy," he says.

I spin around, tightening the knot of my sarong around my waist. "Ryan."

"You're gonna pay for leaving me with Timmy boy." He tries to tickle me, and it brings me back to being a kid. Let me explain something, I'm so ticklish, you can point a finger at me and I will laugh. And if you tickle me, I will cross over into that zone of laughing so hard no sound comes out. Ryan knows this and used my Achilles heel to his advantage on many occasions to get what he wanted or to punish me. It's tickle torture. I hate it, but here I am laughing because it's uncontrollable.

I laugh and squeal, trying my hardest to get away before he can make contact with my ribs. "Stop. Ok, ok, please," I beg, swatting at his large hands.

He doesn't let up until he's moved me down the walk, and we end up at the railing at the furthest spot from the beach. Finally, he stops his playful torture, and we both turn to gaze out at the endless ocean.

"It's beautiful isn't it?" I ask.

"Yeah," he breathes. He grabs my hand, rubbing the pad of his thumb over my skin.

"You do realize I totally won, right?"

He drops my hand, and I instantly miss the touch. "What? No way," he protests. "I had high score,"

I raise a brow at him. "You cheated."

"Did not."

"Did too, Ryan. Oh wait, are you going to cry? You're going to cry, aren't you?" I tease.

He picks me up, hauling me halfway over the side, his hands firm against my skin. "Take it back, or into the water with you foul wench," he says in a pirate's voice. More like a Captain Jack Sparrow voice, but all the same.

"Ryan," I scream, and he wiggles me slightly, dangling me over the edge.

"Admit defeat," he says in a deep voice.

"Never," I shout.

He sets me down, but his hands still hold my hips, his fingers pressing into my skin ever so gently. The wind whips at my hair, and the only thing rooting me to the weathered, wooden boards beneath my feet is my pounding heart. Clouds drift over the sun, blocking it out, and I study his shadowed face. His eyes are beautiful. A soft shade of green, like a meadow on a warm summer's day. What must they have seen at war? They're scarred with the memory he tries his hardest to cover up.

Something else is there, too. A twinkle of desire with an underlayer of fear.

Without thought, I reach my hand to his stubbled jaw, caressing his taut skin with my shaky fingers.

The world around us quiets in the moment. Gone are the giggling children down by the shore. Gone are the chattering ladies, begging their husbands to go home after a long day of fishing. The only thing here and now are the beating hearts of two friends. Two friends who mean the world to each other.

It's with that thought I drop my hand and step away. I just got him back in my life. There's no way I'd be an idiot and ruin that. Sure, it's all about the friendship and has absolutely nothing to do with the sinking feeling he doesn't feel the same. If I put my heart on the line and he turns me down...I'd never be able to cope with that.

So, I push myself off the ledge my back is welded against and make my way down the boardwalk and onto the beach.

Ryan follows closely behind, and we spend the next few hours in friend mode, once again pretending things are as they've always been. When the sun goes down and night falls, we decide to head home. He turns to me in the lot before I hop on my trusty little Vespa. "Ok, you win," he surprises me by saying. "I'll pick you up Saturday night."

"Oh ok. I, uh, yeah ok."

"You don't have a date, do you? I'm sorry," he apologizes. "I'm a jackass. I shouldn't have assumed you were free. It's ok, we can hang out another time."

"I don't have a date," I say, firmly. Not anymore. Connor doesn't even register on the Richter scale of people I want to spend my Saturday night with.

His boyish grin graces his face, and oh how adorable it is. "Ok, I'll pick you up at eight."

"I'll be ready."

Before we can get any further, a group of guys walk around the corner into the dark lot, lit only by a single small light pole.

I'm not afraid until they are right on top of us, four guys all asking us for spare change.

"Here you go." Ryan pulls out a dollar from his pocket.

I watch the exchange, quietly, and my heart races.

"Is that all you got?" the guy sneers.

Ryan grabs my arm, moving me behind him. "Yeah, that's it. Have a great night. " He then turns to me. "I'll take you home."

"Ok," I whisper.

Ryan moves to open his truck door, and I step closer to him.

"Where you going? We just want to talk to you," another man says, stepping closer to Ryan.

"Not tonight. I need to get my girl home."

My face grows hot. Could be fear or it could be the fact that Ryan just called me his girl.

The man charges at Ryan, and I scream. In the flash of an eye, Ryan has him on the ground. Agony twists the man's face. And then I see it, Ryan has his finger twisted into an unnatural position. The look on his face is one I've never seen before. It's the look of a trained killer.

"I'm a marine." Icy wintergreen eyes challenge the others in the group. "Trust me, you don't want a part of this. Now back the fuck off."

The man on his knees gapes up to Ryan in fear, while the other guys inch forward. Oh hell no. If they think they're about to jump Ryan, they're mistaken. As the saying goes, I might be little, but I'm fierce. Sort of. I think? We'll find out. I take my keys, and let the sharp point stick out between my pointer and middle finger. Seems like I read that somewhere.

"You heard him," I say.

Ryan releases the man's finger, and he stands. "Back the fuck up," Ryan warns.

I swear Ryan grows three sizes larger while he squares off with these guys. The more I stare at them, I realize, they're young.

Probably fresh out of high school. I could definitely have taken these fuckers.

They all run off, and Ryan waits a while making sure they don't come back.

"What exactly were you going to do, Lizzy?" Ryan asks, spinning around to face me. A muscle ticks in his chiseled jaw.

"I don't know," I tell him, "but surely you didn't think I would just stand there and let them hurt you."

"You were going to protect me, huh?" he says, crossing his arms.

"Yes, actually," I reply, crossing my arms.

"Protect *yourself* if you're ever in that position," he says with such force, it nearly moves me from spot. "You kick, you scream, go for the eyes, their dick. Whatever you have to do. But do not," he grits out through clenched teeth, "put yourself in danger for me. Because if something happened to you, I don't know what I would do."

My breath catches. "Same here," I say, softly. He's still pissed, but I'm not going to lie and say I wouldn't do it again. I mean, it's not like anyone even paid attention to what I said anyways. "Glad we settled this," I say, climbing on my Vespa.

"I'll follow you home," he says as I strap on my helmet.

"Ok. And thank you."

"Lizzy, you're always safe with me."

I nod. After seeing what he did, I'd say that's pretty damn accurate.

CHAPTER 7

CRYIN'

> Stand up for something, even if it means standing alone.

Therapy is a drag, even if I get to spend time with my favorite person. When I left the service with an injury, it was non-stop doctors' visits and treatment centers. And, of course, you can't forget the psych evaluations.

My time in Afghanistan is a never-ending reminder to how fragile life truly is. Making my way up the steps of the physical treatment center, Lizzy's blonde hair flowing in the breeze on the beach the other afternoon is the only thing I can think about. When did her hair become my obsession? Not until recently did I view the untamed waves as sex hair.

There were so many times I wanted to lean in and kiss her. Grip the long strands in my fist and tug. Hell, I'd have been happy just brushing the hair away from her face while we stood on that busted old boardwalk.

Continuing to put myself in her tempting presence is probably not a good idea. My shoulder feels much better since her deep tissue massage, and I wish that could be the end of therapy.

I pull open the glass door and step inside, letting the air conditioning cool my overheated skin. Going anywhere in the dead heat of summer is always a drag here in Florida, but the AC makes it all better when it hits your body. I spot Lizzy by the reception desk.

There she is. The little nurse who could. She's adorable in scrubs. Today they're a soft blue, matching the summer sky.

The office buzzes with senseless chatter from patients in the room awaiting their turn.

I sign in with the nurse upfront and take a seat.

Lizzy waves and then heads through a door, lost from my vision.

I'm not in the mood to be here today. I have a slight headache again, and my irritability from the dull ache is something I don't want to deal with anymore.

I rub at my temples, easing the pain away.

Lizzy calls my name, and I stand, cracking my neck to the side to ward off the headache that is getting worse by the second.

"How are you feeling?" she asks, once we are tucked away in her little room.

"Fine. I guess."

She scrunches her nose, her eyes narrowing. "You're tense."

"Maybe."

She looks down at my chart, making notes. "Lie down. We'll start with a massage. Then, maybe we'll do some ROM exercises."

"ROM?" I ask.

"Range of motion. Don't worry, you'll feel better when you leave here today. Maybe surfing wasn't the best idea." She sets my chart down, gazing up at me with her soft brown eyes.

"Surfing is always a good idea." I take off my shirt and toss it onto the nearby chair and get into position on the table. Soft music filters in the room, and I close my eyes. The minute her hands make contact with my skin, I moan. Fuck. I'm sure that's frowned upon, but the way she touches me feels so damn good.

She continues on as if the moan was perfectly normal, and I relax as her hands work into the muscles aching in my shoulder.

The music take me away to a different time.

The dust settles around me as I gaze out into the nothingness of the desert. The sun barrels down on me, making it impossible to think clearly. A loud whistle sounds through the air. RPG. Fuck.
My commanding officer shouts, and the boom of the impact sounds in the distance.
"Down, Wagner," he yells.
My head is foggy, and there's a distinct smell in the air making me nauseous.
My buddy, Davis, comes up from behind me and tackles me to the ground as another rocket makes impact. This time it hits a nearby Humvee. Shit. I lift my head. Sand in my eyes makes it hard to see before Davis's hand presses my head firmly back down.
We set out this morning for a routine drive into another camp. When our Humvee blew a gasket, our platoon had to stop.
Now, here we are, fifteen men, stuck on the side of the road, surrounded by rockets launching and exploding.
I lift my head once more.
My friends are everywhere—some screaming, some running.
"Dude, we need to get to the Humvee," Davis says.
I don't need to be told twice.
We move fast as gunfire in the distance sounds off.
"To the vehicles," Sergeant Haines shouts.
Honestly, I'm not sure if the vehicles are a good idea. One Humvee broken down, another blown away.
But, I obey orders, no matter if I agree or not.

Davis and I run. One false move and we get taken out. I won't let it happen today. Not on my last week here.
My tour here in Afghanistan is almost over. Getting my ass stateside is my primary goal.
Davis opens the door, and I hit the steel floorboard.

"Ryan?" Lizzy's voice echoes from far away.

I shake my dizzy head, my vision blurring slightly. "Did I fall asleep?"

She smiles, warm and friendly. "You did. I guess you were really tired."

"I guess so. I feel better though. My headache is practically gone."

"Good. Let's move you to another room to do some exercises."

I hop off the table and put my shirt back on, following her out of the room.

A while later when I'm home, I debate telling anyone about the headache I experienced today. It was most likely just the summer heat getting to me.

My phone buzzes with a text from Devin.

Mom said to get your ass over here if you want to eat, pretty boy.

Knowing she'll just show up if I don't, I make my way to their house.

Walking into my childhood home, memories assault me of wrestling with my brothers and playing board games late into the evening with my family at the coffee table. Things have changed. Instead of the giant lace doily covering the top when I was a kid, surfing magazines and remote controls adorn it. My mother used to shudder at the sight of magazines draped all over the large house. Now, it appears she's finally given into the madness of living with a house full of men.

The aroma of pasta sauce enters my nose, and I breathe deep, loving my mother's secret ingredient she uses to make the best sauce I've ever had. Definitely beats any meal I ever had in the mess hall while in the service.

I kiss my mother's cheek, then grab a beer from the fridge. Everything has changed so much since I was kid. All new stainless steel appliances decorate the space, and gone are the yellow curtains that hung over the window showcasing the back yard. In their place are white blinds which remain shut.

My brothers chat away at the large, oak table off to the end of the kitchen.

I grab a seat across from them at the table.

"This wave was astronomical in size, dude," Lance tells Devin, and I zone out.

My mind strays to Lizzy, wondering what she's doing and thinking about her quirky habits. Like the way she can only eat three jelly beans at a time. Oh, and they all have to be red. The way she belts out the wrong lyrics to songs. Her complete passion for anything pertaining to celestial bodies in space.

For years, I'd sit with her in her backyard gazing through a telescope at a bunch of tiny white dots in the night sky. She'd go on and on about the constellations and even tell me the names of each tiny speck.

Does anyone know these things? Does anyone else know that when she sleeps she has to be bundled with covers from head to toe? Or that she eats one thing at a time on her plate?

I know these things, yet, I don't know her like I used to. Maybe she no longer eats only red jellybeans and has graduated to other colors.

"Earth to Cryin'?" Lance says.

"Don't call me that," I grit out.

"You coming to hear me play tomorrow night?" Devin asks.

"Yeah, sure. We'll see."

Only the next night I don't go see him play. I lie in bed with a headache that could move mountains.

A migraine of all migraines and I close my eyes tight wishing the pain away.

I peer at my cell, knowing if anything will help soothe this ache, it'll be Lizzy's sexy voice. I dial and wait for her to pick up.

"Hey, soldier," she coos.

Already my headache eases. "Hey." I think back to her skimpy pink bikini and reposition myself flat on my back on the bed. "What are you up to?"

"Just getting into bed. I have a busy day tomorrow."

"Oh yeah?" My dick twitches at the image that forms in my mind of a scantily clad Lizzy in bed. "Well obviously I have to ask what you're wearing now," I tease her. But I'm fucking serious.

She laughs. "A pink tank and sleep shorts with stars."

My pulse quickens. Fuck. Why did I ask? That might be sexier than the bikini.

I change the subject. "Sorry to be calling so late."

"It's ok. Are you alright?" she asks.

Sitting up, I take off my shirt, lying back down in nothing but my boxer briefs. "Yeah. I just wanted to hear your voice."

"Well, I'm glad you called. I've been thinking about you all day."

My ears perk up, like a dog in heat, and my body reacts in sort of the same fashion. "Oh yeah? Why's that?"

"I was thinking about the other night, with those guys. How badass you were."

I smile. "It was nothing. In the military they trained us for everything."

"Were you ever scared over there?" Her voice drops, and I imagine her lying in her bed, her wild hair splayed all over the pillow.

"Sometimes. When we went under attack, I really thought I'd never make it home."

"I'm so glad you did," she says, softly. "I'd miss you too much if you didn't."

She's turning me on. It isn't even the conversation, just her sexy breaths and voice that's doing a number on me. "Why?" I want to bring her to the point of saying she wants me, even if I know she doesn't. There's safety in the night with her on the other end of the phone.

Bravery is something I've never had to question. I had no problems rushing into an enemy camp or fighting. But, right now, I feel like a coward waiting with baited breath hoping she says something, anything, to show me she wants me.

"I'd miss how much fun we have together. I'd miss having someone to talk to."

"I'm sure Big Red would keep you company." Jealousy hits me.

"Oh please. He doesn't do it for me." She laughs and it's the sweetest sound.

"Yeah, that's right. I remember what gets you going." I close my eyes. "You have witchcraft in your lips," I say, quoting Shakespeare.

She inhales sharply. "I love Shakespeare. And, you're right. It does get me going."

My dick jumps, hardening at her words. "Oh yeah? Are you turned on right now?"

She hesitates before answering, "I can't tell you that."

Fuck. She is. "Tell me. It's just two friends talking about what gets them going."

"Ok, well, your turn. What does it for you? What gets your blood pumping." she asks.

I rub a hand over my cock. "Pink bikinis." I take a deep breath. "In my heart there was a kind of fighting that would not let me sleep," I say, quoting another Shakespeare line.

"Oh damn. Great line." Silence fills the line, and then, "Is it true? Are you fighting with something?"

I debate on telling her how true that line is. My mind fights. My heart is in a battle of a lifetime. And my soul is nowhere near peace. Between her beauty and the want I have for her mixed with the hell I face everyday, and the dwindling hopes for a happy life, yes, I am at war.

"No, I'm fine," I answer. My mood sours and the headache returns. "Listen, I know you work tomorrow. I should let you go."

"Oh, ok."

"I'll see you soon." After she says goodbye, I hang up, close my eyes, and try to sleep.

∽

By Saturday I'm feeling great. Lizzy calls to tell me to be ready for a fun night, and already I know this can't be good.

Whenever she mentions fun, I know she's planning something that'll most likely be torture for me.

As promised, I pick her up at eight.

She steps out wearing a pale, blue dress that floats around her silky legs. Legs I can't stop staring at. But, the short length of the dress isn't even the best part. It's the way the bodice holds her tits close, creating the perfect cleavage to run my tongue between.

In her hands is her trusty telescope. The one I haven't seen since we were kids.

"Ready to go?" She smiles. God, her fucking smile is what every man most likely fantasizes about at night. I do.

"Yeah," I whisper, and already, I'm having a hard time pushing the sexual thoughts of her away.

"Head to the pier," she directs, when I back out of her driveway.

"Sure thing." I spin the wheel in the direction of the beach. "Let's grab something to eat first."

A few hours later, with a large, silky sheet spread out, and the telescope set up a few feet away, we sit underneath a blanket of stars along the warm sand, chatting about the old days.

"I've missed this," Lizzy says, adjusting the knobs on her telescope.

There's nowhere else I'd rather be than on this sheet, my legs stretched out, observing her gaze at the heaven's above. "Me too," I tell her. "I've missed everything."

She lifts her head from the eyepiece. "Come here."

I obey, rising to my feet and making my way closer to her. "What am I looking for?"

She points to the telescope. "Just look."

I was never able to see what she could looking at the sky, but I bend my head, lining my eye up with the telescope. Again, all I see are a bunch of tiny specks of lights all clustered together. She lifts my hand placing it on the knob, gently guiding my hand to bring them into focus. "Oh ok," I say, still not really sure what I'm supposed to be seeing.

"Gorgeous, isn't it?"

I lift my head. "Yeah," I murmur, gazing at her.

The air around us zaps and sizzles with an odd unfamiliarity. I find myself wanting to spend every moment with her.

Sure, we were inseparable as kids, but this is more.

Every morning I wake to thoughts of her, and when I close my eyes at night she's all I see.

I turn away from her and return to the sheet, taking a seat under the pale moonlight. The secluded beach is quiet this late at night, and I take the opportunity to ogle her as she resumes her stance over the telescope.

"Looking for the Cryin' Lizard?"

"Maybe," she says. And then, then, if I wasn't tormented enough, the breeze lifts her skirt, teasing me with a view of her rounded ass wearing light blue panties to match her sundress.

Fuck. My dick stirs to life. I run my fingers through the sand, lying on my side, hoping for another glimpse.

She turns to me, ending any chance of that happening. "Can I ask you something?"

"Sure." I sit up a little, waiting for her next words.

"When you were in the military, did you have to follow orders no matter what?"

I crack a small smile. "Yeah."

"I would love to have that job." She leaves the telescope and sits down next to me, crossing her legs at the ankles.

"What? Bossing people around?"

Her eyes meet mine. "No, just bossing you around."

I laugh. "Is that so? Go ahead. What would you have me do?"

"Oh really? You're going to let me be your commanding officer?" She gets excited, perching up onto her knees.

"Sure, why not?" I stand, because if I don't, I'm going to haul her into my lap and ravage her mouth with my tongue. Grind her pussy on me until she begs me to fuck her.

She purses her lips, bringing her finger to them, thinking. "Let's see, Private Wagner. Why not take off your shoes, and run out and get your toes wet."

I cock a brow. "Really?" I was hoping for something more sexual.

"Yes." She smiles, big. Like a kid in a candy shop, excited to get their reward.

I do as she says, running to the water's edge and getting my feet wet in the cold ocean. "Oh, fuck, that's cold."

She laughs from the safety back on shore.

I dip my hands in the water, cupping a small amount in my palms and race back to where she's seated and trickle it down the back of her neck.

"Shit, Ryan." She's on her feet in no time, and I tickle her back to the ground. Hovering over her, her flat on her back, my smile drops. I want her so fucking bad.

"You're supposed to be doing as I say," she whispers.

Our eyes slam into each other, and my heart beats a thunderous rhythm. "Give me another order." My voice is low, soft, and I pray she doesn't ask me to get off her.

"Kiss me, Ryan."

And, I fucking do. To hell with friendship.

Our lips meet, and my hands dive into her wild hair as she claws at my back. I kiss her hard and deep, claiming every inch of her perfect mouth.

She gasps as I nibble at her bottom lip, and moans as my hand traces down her body, lifting her leg over my back.

I press my thickening dick against her center letting her grind against me.

The crashing waves are the soundtrack to our kiss, playing on repeat as I go further pulling the top of her dress down a bit to kiss the swells of her breasts and finally run my tongue through the valley between them. She doesn't want me to stop, urging me on by gripping her fingers into my hair. But, what if I don't?

Lizzy's my best friend. I shouldn't be here with her. I shouldn't be thinking about all the filthy things I want to do to her right now. Wondering what she looks like, what she sounds like, when she comes.

I break the kiss, sitting up in the process. "I'm sorry, Lizzy."

My hands tug at my short hair as she lies there, not saying anything. I'm selfish.

She had a life before I came crashing back into it. Instead of restoring our friendship, I might destroy it forever.

She could never love someone like me. An injured soldier.

She deserves better.

∼

CHAPTER 8

LIZARD

> He had beautiful eyes. The kind you could get lost in; and I guess I did.

Wow. So that's what it's like to really kiss Ryan Wagner. The kiss he just laid on me was better than any kiss fantasy I've ever had. Even the fantasy involving Chris Hemsworth, which is very hard to outdo. But, Ryan surpassed anything I could have ever imagined.

I was being so good, gazing at Orion's Belt and the Seven Sisters star constellations, minding my own business.

Now everything is all uncomfortable, awkward, and weird.

I wish I could say something, but I think he kissed my lips into numbness. I may never get the use of my lips back ever again.

Ah, to walk the world, affected forever from his kiss. Which if I'm being honest, I'm sure his kiss will affect me in other ways for the rest of my life.

It was everything a kiss should be. Passionate. Carnal. I know.

I know. I'm non-stop talking about this kiss, but well, you would too if you'd just been kissed like I had.

Don't be jealous, though, because right now, as I peer over to Ryan, he appears like I was his worst mistake. And it's a horrible feeling. My silly crush I've always harbored, is always going to be just that. A silly crush.

And, I can't fucking think of a thing to say, so I deflect, or I'm going to cry. "Alnitak, Alnilam, and Mintaka," I recite, barely above a whisper.

Ryan turns to face me, a small smile playing at his lips. "I'm sorry? Are you speaking English?"

Even though it hurts, I smile back. "Sorry, it was the first thing that popped in my head."

"Oh, right. It happens," he shrugs, "most girls I kiss usually start speaking in tongues afterwards.

My heart sinks at all the other girls he's kissed. Did mine rate up there with the others? I hide my insecurity under a veil of laughter and slap his shoulder. "It isn't gibberish. It's the name of the three stars in Orion's Belt." I point to the constellation with my finger and Ryan's green eyes follow, gazing up into the night sky.

"Ah, sure."

"You can Google if you don't believe me," I defend myself.

"No, I would never doubt you. You're the star expert." He runs a hand on the backside of his neck. All cute and sweet like, and my heart squeezes. I don't want him to feel strange around me now and ease out of my life. I'd rather hurt everyday being around him than let him go again.

"Ok, listen, about the kiss, Ryan. It was sweet." Oh God, I sound ridiculous. "I mean, it was nice."

He appears dejected. "Ouch, nice, huh?"

Our eyes meet and my cheeks heat. "I mean it was good." I should stop talking.

And then, like a rocket, Ryan's lips attack mine. And it is

anything but nice, sweet, or good. No, the kiss he lays on me is rough, hard, digging into me with a fierceness neither of us can contain.

His fingers shove into my skin. My hands tug him closer.

Magic happens in the evening. Like right now, invisible glitter and stardust cascades from the sky, covering us with its beauty.

It's the starting of the fall.

The fall into each other.

My only fear is that Ryan doesn't feel the same way.

I'm being silly. Of course, he doesn't.

The evening makes you do crazy things.

Things a sane person wouldn't do.

Because, magic lives here, in the evening...and tomorrow when the dust settles, and the sun rises...it'll all be over.

The kiss ends.

And I'm disoriented.

His eyes are hazy with lust. "Lizzy, I'm sorry. I just didn't want to be a less than stellar kisser."

"Stellar. Nice word choice. It also relates to the stars, which isn't how you meant it. But, " I ramble. "Yeah, no, you're cool." I hop to my feet, scrambling to gather everything together to head home. Home. Where it's safe from feelings.

Feelings I've held in for years.

Feelings which are all slowly seeping from every pore of my body.

Ryan follows suit and gathers the last of our belongings, and we both head in silence to his truck. After loading the telescope in the back, we hop into the cab and he drives toward my house.

Silence.

More silence.

Now it's an awkward silence.

I grow frustrated and turn in my seat to face him. "Ryan, I think we should talk about what happened."

I mean, shouldn't we?

He pulls off the side of Atlantic Ave, slamming his foot on the brake. At this dark hour, the street is seemingly deserted. The occasional car passes, beaming their lights through the window of Ryan's truck. In this neighborhood with private school children, and white picket fences I'm not worried about anything bad happening. Unless you count what I'm about to do. I'm going to lay it on the line.

"Ok, talk," he orders, with one hand gripping the black steering wheel, tightly.

I gaze at his fingers, remembering how just a while ago they were wrapped through my long hair, and suck in a deep breath. "Well, I think it was a mistake. I mean, we're friends, right?" Oh God, why is this so hard? Part of me hopes he'll confess to wanting me as much as I want him. Maybe, just maybe, he feels the same. I've left the door cracked for him, giving him the opportunity to swing it wide open.

He nods. "Yeah, you're right. I shouldn't have kissed you. I..."

I cut in, "No, it's ok. I shouldn't have asked." I don't want to hear his regret.

This conversation couldn't be more awkward. I wish he'd just start the car and take me home so I can forget about this night.

As if he can read my thoughts, he fires up the ignition and speeds down the road.

When he pulls into my driveway, he offers very little chit chat, and I rush to get my things as he helps me bring my telescope inside.

We say goodbye, and he pulls away, taking a little piece of my heart with him.

∼

After the discomfort of the other night, I haven't called or seen Ryan. In all honesty, I don't really know what to say to him.

But, that will soon change since he has an appointment today, and again I'll get to feel his muscles as I give him a massage.

My fingers tremble with nerves. This is more excruciating than losing my virginity at sixteen with Grant Middleton in his father's garage after school. He had eaten a bag of Cheetos, so it wasn't a pleasant experience. I remember being terrified of getting caught and repulsed at his Cheeto breath and orange fingertips.

Now, even though Ryan and I both agreed it was a mistake kissing, I'm still anxious. If I'm being honest, I didn't think it was a mistake at all. Why would he kiss me like that? He didn't have to go all in. Why would he? Maybe it's because Ryan has been in the service a while. He probably hasn't had sex in the four years he was away, so I'm sure he's extra horny. Horny enough to kiss his best friend as if his life depended on it. Ok, I know it wasn't prison, but I'm sure he didn't have women flirting with him day in and day out.

He steps through the front door of the office, and all eyes are on him. Quiet and stillness settles over the waiting room as everyone gapes at him. Maybe not everyone, but I know I sure am. He has a presence about him, and it's as if he owns the room.

He steps up to the reception desk, signs the white paper attached to the clipboard, and takes a seat against the wall.

From my position in the back office, he can't see me, and I prefer it this way. I need a minute to compose myself before I call him back to my tiny room.

Smoothing the top of my scrubs down, I walk to the door and call out his name. His smile lights me up inside, and all the awkwardness from the other night melts away.

"Hi," he says when he's close enough for me to hear.

I smile. "Hey."

We step into my room, and he removes his shirt right on cue and hops on the table.

I dim the lights, turning on the soft music, and add a dab of lotion to my hands. Focusing on a piece of artwork decorating the far wall, I zero in on the constellations gazing back at me. Ryan's shoulders are tense as I knead into them. Closing my eyes, I focus on the feel of his soft skin under my fingertips. His muscles relax under my pressure. For one fleeting moment, I wish I could leave this room, this little oasis of soft music and gentle, pastel colored walls, and take him back to my house and do wicked things with him.

But, I control my hormones, and focus on the task at hand...that is, until he moans. The simplest of sounds raises my internal temperature and has my heart beating wildly inside my chest.

I pause, and he sits up.

"Lizzy, I'm sorry. Your hands...they're turning me the fuck on."

I stare down at my hands and see his cock jutting forward in his shorts. "I'm sorry. Maybe we should stop for today and do a few exercises instead?"

He grabs my hand from his seated position. "Not yet."

I'm speechless as I get lost in his stare. This is wrong, he's my friend. We shouldn't cross this line again, even if I want to.

The mood is set—dim lights, flowy music. Almost reminds me of a high school dance. Except the only dancing here is around the question whether or not this means something.

I'm at work, and this isn't the place to put my feelings to the test. Especially with Ryan.

As well as my brain knows this, my body is slow on the take.

I ignite under his gaze. His intensity overwhelms me, makes my panties wet, and I take a deep breath.

Ryan was my sounding board. My saving grace growing up. He was there for me in my darkest hour when things went south with my parents. And, even though I want him to kiss me again, I don't want to lose our friendship when things sour. Which, they always do. Just look at my parents. Once, so in love, and then one day it all came crashing down and ended in divorce.

So, with nerves of steel and confidence of stone I'm doing the right thing, I turn away from him. I don't want him to regret me again. "Let's do some ROM exercises."

He hops down from the table, making his way to the wood door. "Sure," he whispers.

The next hour is not as uncomfortable as I thought it would be. Ryan and I fall back into our best friend groove, and I help him work out his shoulder.

At the end of the session, after many laughs and jokes, he says he'll call me later to hang out. And, I wish for one tiny second it could be more than it is.

CHAPTER 9

CRYIN'

" Make love, not war

Fuck, I need to keep my head in the game. Being with Lizzy is not an option. She deserves better, not a fucked-up war vet like me.

No, Lizzy deserves the best things life has to offer.

After leaving the doctor's office, I drive into town, stopping at a small bar within the city limits of Miami.

When I step through the wooden doors, I'm transported back in time. Annoying neon lights flash against an oval, frosted-glass bar. The music is even straight out of the 1980's. It's all a bit ridiculous, but as I examine the few people who are out on a weekday, they appear to be enjoying themselves.

I park myself on a vinyl red stool and order an Old Fashioned. The muscle-clad bartender muddles the orange, cherries, and sugar, and my mind wanders back to her. She would love it here. Retro and nostalgic. She'd be dancing like all the girls up on stage right now. But she'd look way better than the primadonnas up there now. Lizzy with her wild hair bumping and grinding to Boy George, what a sight that would be.

Downing my drink, I wonder what the fuck I'm doing with my life. The open enrollment for school has ended with me not even signing up for a semester. Working for my father is cool, but I can't do it for much longer.

It doesn't really matter anyway; life goes on, whether you plan for it or not.

~

"Cover your left eye and read the fourth line down," Dr. James says, as I stand in his stark white office again. It feels like a frozen tundra with how cold it is and how icy I feel inside.

I cover my eye, repeating what I see, "L, P, E, B."

He marks furiously in my patient chart. "Third line."

"T, O, Z."

"Very good." He stands in front of me, pressing along my temples. "Any headaches?"

"Nope, none." I smile, hoping he believes me. The last two headaches were nothing…just the heat, I'm sure.

"How's therapy going for that shoulder?" he asks.

"Good. It rarely hurts at all." Now *that* is the truth, thanks to Lizzy's magic fingers.

I leave his office with another follow up appointment scheduled. The Florida sun shines bright overhead, casting a shadow that follows me back to my father's surf shop, back into work. This should be any surfer's dream job, but for me…I'm not so sure. I always felt like I was destined for so much more. It's one of the reasons I joined the military—to protect and serve.

Old habits die hard, and with military precision, I count off the klicks to my father's shop…three klicks, three thousand meters.

Fresh air hits my face. Florida is full of sea and salt in the air; a mist of humidity on your skin. I would have given my left nut for a droplet of water in the air in Afghanistan. It was dry, dusty, sandy, and downright hot as hell.

After going through the motions at work, I dash through the now pouring rain and enter my bungalow. The pungent smell of lemons makes my eyebrows scrunch together. Knowing damn well my mother has been over to clean, I head off to the kitchen to see her efforts.

Just as I thought, the bright stainless steel appliances and granite countertops glisten beneath the overhead light. I'm not a slob by any means. As a matter of fact, the 1500 square feet of my home are usually pristine thanks to the military. The sand colored tile throughout is clean enough to eat off of. She still likes to feel "needed," and this is her way of doing it, I guess.

I flick on the TV, and settle in the leather recliner to watch Lance's surfing competition from last spring. A knock at the door breaks my attention from the show, and I answer to find a dripping wet Lizzy. "Can I come in?" she asks with a slight shiver to her voice.

"Yeah, of course." I snap into action, moving out of the way and down the hallway. "Let me get you a towel."

She follows me, rubbing her arms to warm up. "Thanks."

"What are you doing? Playing in the rain?"

She eyes me sideways. "Very funny. I had to see you."

I grab a thick, yellow towel for her and hand it over. She pulls her hair through it, wringing it out.

"Had to see me? Why?"

"I need your help," she says, moving toward the kitchen to sit on a stool at the bar.

"Sure, ok. What's up?" I slam my hands in the pockets of my worn-out jeans, waiting for her response.

She hmm's and ah's before she finally spits it out, "Connor asked me out again," she says.

"What did you say?" I move closer.

"Well, I said yes."

I crack a smile, hating she's going out with him. "Is he going to recite Shakespeare the whole night?"

She looks down at the floor, then back at me. "No, I actually think that might be kind of cool."

Jealousy, like a machine gun, fires off inside of me. "Right. Because it gets you going." I want to break his fucking hands so he can't put them on her.

"No, I didn't mean that," she denies.

I nudge her knees open and step between them. Towering over her, I lean in until our noses almost touch. "For where thou art, there is the world itself. And where thou art not, desolation."

She sucks in a breath, her eyes closing, and I want to touch her.

Move away. Don't do it.

But I can no longer heed my brain's commands. My hand reaches forward, tucking a loose strand of her hair behind her ear.

Her lids spring open, and the truths hidden behind her irises are overwhelming.

She wants me. She wants this. But just like me she's afraid.

And, just like me she won't cross that line.

But, fuck, I want to.

She leans into my touch. Her skin is soft against my rough palm.

My cock jumps, wanting only her. Needing only her.

"Lizzy," I whisper.

"Do it, Ryan. Just do it."

God, I wish I could, but I can't. My hand falls from her face, and I back away to gaze into her eyes—serious and amber-colored with beautiful specks of gold.

It's so hard to resist her, but I do it. "Let's watch a movie."

"Sure," she says, rising and brushing past me.

We move to the couch, sitting side by side, and I start a movie we both loved growing up—*We Were Soldiers*. My shoulder aches, and Lizzy notices my discomfort.

"Here, come sit on the floor between my legs. I'll rub your shoulder."

She doesn't have to ask me twice.

I do as told, and she gets to work, kneading my muscles into nirvana. It feels so good. Her hands roam all down my back sending waves of pleasure straight to my dick. I'm getting turned on, and I try to think about anything but her.

Gaskets, fuel pumps, and spark plugs of the Humvees we drove overseas. Hot days, sand in my eyes, and working all day on broken engines, hoping they'd make it across the desert. All these things flood my brain, but they're no match for Lizzy's hands on me.

Every push and pull ignites desire in my body.

Think car parts. Think about that goddamn desert. Think about anything.

But, it's no use. I'm weak for her.

I turn, gazing up into her eyes and forget about the friendship. Forget about trying to not ruin this.

I run my hand up her thigh, and she closes her eyes. Her skin is so soft, and I continue up her shorts just a bit.

She moans, and it urges me on. Rising onto my knees, I add my other hand on her opposite leg.

"Ryan, I've wanted you for a long time," she whispers.

It's like music to my ears when she utters the words. I apply pressure to her legs, massaging, as my lips kiss right above her knee.

Her hands fly into my hair, pulling and tugging me closer to her.

Staring at her right now, with the light from the TV fluttering against her light skin, I've never wanted anyone more.

How could I see her everyday but never truly see her?

She's everything a woman should be. And, she's got the biggest heart I've ever known.

I trace higher up her legs, underneath the denim of her shorts, nearing her center. There's no turning back now.

There's no stopping, even if I tried.

My cock aches to be inside her. To claim her.

To fill her up with passion.

When my lips meet hers, her mouth opens for me, allowing my tongue to run along hers. She's the sweetest kisser.

I'm being a greedy bastard, but for now I don't care. I'll worry about the consequences of my actions later. After I've felt every part of her.

Her hands trace down my back, tugging my shirt over my head. When she lifts my shirt off, she sucks in a breath. Soft kisses tickle my chest and arms, and my hands pull at the button on her jean shorts.

"Lizzy, I've never wanted anything more in my life."

She smiles, and already it breaks my heart. A heart she's slowly claiming with every glance, touch, and smile.

It breaks my heart because I know it won't last. Tomorrow will be a new day, and I'll come to terms with the fact that she deserves better than me. She deserves a man who's not scarred from the war.

A man who can give her a life she's always wanted.

But, tonight, I don't care about any of those reasons.

No, tonight she's mine.

Tonight, I'll picture the life her and I could have had.

If things weren't fucked up.

∽

CHAPTER 10

LIZARD

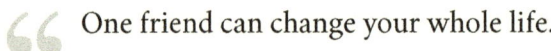 One friend can change your whole life.

The way he touches me sets my skin ablaze. Everything he does is so right. The way he lifts me in his arms. How he carries me back to his room and tosses me on the bed like I'm a ragdoll. The way he steps back, running his finger along his jaw, as his intense stare is fixed on me.

"Take your clothes off. Let me see all of you," he says, and my skin tingles with anticipation.

I've imagined this scenario a million times when I was younger. So as my wishes come true, I study him as he stands at the foot of the black, platform bed with his eyes clocking my every move. The time for doubts and insecurities is gone. This is happening, let the pieces of my heart fall where they may.

In ten seconds my clothes are gone, and his eyes fill with desire in the soft light of the moon streaming through the window.

The bed dips as he climbs on, hovering his body on top of mine.

I want to be with him. I want to have a life with him. I can see it all working out, not ending in mayhem like my parents. No, this could work.

A silent wish is made on the light of a faraway star. I cling to the hope that tomorrow things won't change. That my best friend won't regret crossing the line from friends to lovers.

My moans intensify when his hot mouth trails kisses down my neck. He pushes off his jeans. Sitting up, he lowers his boxers, and I prop up on my elbows to gain a better look. Oh. My. God.

In all my wildest fantasies, I never pictured Ryan with the package he's offering me.

Long, thick, hard, and perfectly straight, pointing directly at me. I reach for it, my hands wrapping around the base.

The sexy sound he makes, bordering on a groan, as I lower my head to capture the tip between my lips spurs me on. I lick my tongue, swirling it, further down his shaft.

His hands race through my hair, clenching it tight within his fists. I've not given a lot of blow jobs, but I'm about to give him one he'll never forget. Looking up at him, I take him further in my mouth as his head falls back, eyes shutting.

Pumping, licking, sucking, with both my hands and mouth, I give him the best blow job I can. Men are really at your mercy when you give them head. Feeling powerful with the way his thighs tremble and he thrusts into my mouth, I give his balls some attention.

"Fuck," he grits out when I gently suck them into my mouth.

That's all the confirmation I need that I'm doing everything right. I lick my way back up and he groans, loud, as I bob my head, his length hitting the back of my throat. My pussy aches with need for him.

"Lizzy, baby, I can't take much more. I need you." He tugs my hair, pulling my mouth from his throbbing cock.

"Then take me, Ryan. I'm yours." I lay flat on my back, waiting for him to sheath a condom over his dick.

He climbs my body, kissing my skin and stopping at my breasts. Ah, god. I can't control the moan that escapes when he sucks a nipple in between his lips, tugging gently with his teeth. My back arches, and I wrap my legs around his hips.

He lines himself up with me and enters me in one, slow push with a drawn out "fuuuuck." My nails dig into his back.

Ah, it feels so good, filling me, stretching me. So big. This is what I've been waiting for. My heart beats so hard, I wonder if he can hear it.

Now I just need him to move, and he does. He rocks, pulling in and out at a steady rhythm.

The simple art of love making turns into fucking with one hard thrust from Ryan. He picks up speed, digging his dick deeper inside me.

It's insane the feelings running rampant through my bones. The longing of wanting him for so long. The satisfaction that it's finally happening.

The madness turns poetic in a sense. Him pounding into me. Hands digging into my hips. Harsh breaths in my ear. The tender way he says my name.

Everything in this moment is exactly what I want for a lifetime.

I cling to his shoulders, squeezing my legs tighter around him. He doesn't let up, and I wouldn't want him to.

I'm all for this ride of a lifetime. Sexual bliss and heat, with passion mixed in, is exactly what I signed up for.

The way his dick feels has my orgasm approaching quickly. I try to stall it, not wanting this night to ever end.

Ryan leans in, claiming my lips once more as my body loses control. I can't take it anymore, and I break the kiss, screaming his name in ecstasy.

A smile lifts his lips as he pushes even deeper. "Fuck, your little pussy is so wet for me." He thrusts harder. "So tight. I like feeling you come all over me."

I want to tell him things. Things no man probably wants to hear while just fucking a friend.

My post orgasmic bliss is ruptured when thoughts of what this was enter my brain at the same time Ryan loses control.

He moans my name, his hands rummaging through my hair, holding on for dear life as his body spasms. When his orgasm subsides, he kisses me, hard, and all of my thoughts melt away. Go with the flow. Don't read too much into this. Wait for him to speak.

He climbs off me, kissing the tip of my nose, before rushing off to the bathroom down the hall. I sit up, pulling the white sheet further up my naked body.

Glancing around his room, I spot the old trophy he and I received in a talent show for an awful performance of The Backstreet Boys song, *Everybody (Backstreets Back)*. I shake my head, laughing, as I make my way over to the wooden shelf where it sits. I trace my fingers over the plated gold bearing our names.

"I'm surprised they didn't throw us out of the contest for how horrible we were," Ryan says, standing at the doorway in a pair of boxer briefs, his finger running along his lower lip.

"Yeah, what were we thinking? I remember thinking how cool we were."

He smiles. "Me too. Remember the move I kept begging to put in the routine, and you kept shooting me down?"

I remember the exact move. "No," I shake my head, "show me."

He moves further into the room and kicks his legs up in a wannabe Michael Jackson dance move mixed with a weird Sia contemporary move as he plays out the choreography.

"I think you're onto something there. Maybe you can quit your father's shop and tour the country as a backup dancer."

He stops, arching a brow. "No, that'll never happen."

I shrug. "You never know."

"I do. I'm destined to work for my father for the time being." He takes two long strides and climbs back into bed. He pats beside him, and I hop in next to him.

"Why do you say that?" I lay my head on his chest, sharing the sheet with him.

"Say what? About my father?" He shrugs. "Just the way things worked out, I guess."

I want to ask him about the war. I want to ask him why he has no desire to go back to school. But, my mouth remains shut.

We lay in silence, neither of us addressing what just happened between us. The big turning stone in our ~~relation,~~ I mean, friendship.

Like the constellation Andromeda, waiting for her hero, Perseus, to save her from the sea. Friends first, then lovers as they traveled back to her home.

Sure, maybe Ryan isn't my Perseus, saving me from a life of not believing in love, but he is someone I would be willing to test the theory on.

I've never been in love before.

The only love I witnessed in my life was my parents. Followed by the misery, torture, and pain when it all fell apart. But, what about Ryan's parents?

They love each other, and you can see it in the little things they do for one another. I haven't seen them in years, but I remember the way her eyes lit up when Mr. Wagner walked into the room.

How he would kiss his wife behind the ear when he thought no one was watching.

Maybe they're the exception, though, and not the rule.

I wake up in a flurry of madness. An alarm ringing, Ryan stirring, and already it's going to be one of *those* days.

"Ryan, wake up. I must go. I'm going to be late for work."

The man doesn't budge. I thought military men were early risers.

Pursing my lips, I nudge his shoulder with my hand. "Ryan." I spot my clothes and put them on as quickly as I can.

Taking one last view of sleepyhead Ryan, I rush out the door and hop into my car. I pull into my driveway, leaning my head on the steering wheel as the realization slams into me of what Ryan and I did last night.

There's no turning back.

I fire off a text to him, so when he wakes up, he knows where I went.

An hour later, I sit in the office at work, replaying every movement, every touch of our..., what would you even call it? Love making? No, not that. Sex? Fucking...no it was more than that, I hope.

With worry and dread, I make it through my workday, afraid to check to see if he texted back. My arms are killing me when I leave work and head out to my car in the empty parking lot. I realize I'm being silly. It's Ryan. He's been a friend for ages. One night of sex won't change that. Or maybe it will.

I survey my phone, and, no, he didn't even reply.

CHAPTER 11

CRYIN'

> There is nothing so powerful as truth, and nothing so strange.

Everyone doesn't know what it's like to be me. To live day in and day out with hell lurking on my doorstep, waiting for the perfect moment to enter. It's like waiting for the storm on a calm, summer's eve. But, I am anything but calm.

I'm terrified.

Knowledge is a scary thing sometimes. It makes you do things you wouldn't normally do.

One night with Lizzy is all I wanted.

One night to hold with me forever. A night I will never forget when it all goes to shit. And I assure you, it will.

I called my father when I woke up alone, and told him I wasn't coming in. Not because I didn't want to, but because my head throbbed with the memory of last night.

I figured Lizzy had rushed off to work, and I was right when I saw her text stating just that. The rest of my day, I paced my apartment, counting steps like they taught us in the military.

Part of me wanted to rush over to Lizzy's when I knew she'd be off work. But, I couldn't make myself dial her number.

Being with her last night was a miracle. Her soft skin, the way she held me close, her lips...God. I fist my fingers through my short hair, and curse loudly.

What the fuck have I done?

I don't want to hurt her, but I can't be with her. She has goals, ambitions, and I would only drag her down.

No one knows what I'm going through. Everyone believes the lie I'm adjusting back into my old life just fine. My parents keep asking me when I'm signing up for courses at the local college. Little do they know the answer is never.

Just last week, my father pulled me aside, in the back room of his shop. Rows and rows of freshly sandpapered boards lined the shelves, and I couldn't break my gaze from them. Neat and orderly with a destination. He asked me what I had planned for my future, and I couldn't answer.

Because what I had planned is completely at odds with what is planned for me.

Sometimes you can't control your own destiny; it's already decided for you.

I end up parking myself on the couch, watching a little TV when there's a knock at my door. Slowly getting up, I open the door and Lizzy waits for me.

She pushes me aside, entering. "Move over, big boy, we're having it out. Kitchen table. Now."

Unsure of what she's doing, I follow her.

"Let's go," she says, sitting in a chair and slamming her elbow on the pine wood.

My mood lightens, like it always does, when she's around. "What are you doing?" I ask, sliding my hands in the pockets of my khaki shorts so I don't grab her and throw her on the table to feast on her sweet pussy.

"Oh, no you don't. Get over here and arm wrestle me." She's very demanding, and I'll be honest...a tad bit scary.

I laugh. "Are you serious?"

"Dead serious. I've been blowing your phone up all evening. You won't return my calls, so we handle this the ol' school way."

When Lizzy and I were kids, and we'd fight, we'd always settle everything over an arm wrestling match.

When we were younger she always gave me a run for my money, but once I gained some muscles she never stood a chance.

"Uh ok. You do realize you're going to lose, right? I mean, look at these guns." I flex my biceps, giving her a peep show to the gun show.

She rolls her eyes. "Oh, please. I've been practicing. I'm really good now."

"Sure." I take a seat across from her, planting my elbow on the table and locking my hand in hers.

"Ready?" she asks.

I nod, and she counts it down.

She's strong, I'll give her that, but please. I win, and her little nose scrunches in anger.

"Fuck, I didn't realize how strong you are," she says, biting the bottom of her lip.

It's this innocent action which weakens me. "I'm sorry I didn't call. Bad day I guess." I rise from my seat and grab a beer from the fridge. "Want one?" I offer her.

She shakes her head. "Want to talk about it?"

"About the beer?" I deflect.

She rolls her eyes again, which turns me on in a major way, and I want to spank her for the action.

"No, your day," she says.

To avoid sounding like a pussy, I ignore her question and head into the living room and park myself on the couch. Sure, I had a bad day. But, what reason could I give her? I was feeling pissed at the world, so I called out of work?

She follows me, sitting beside me. "Come on, Ry. We used to tell each other everything."

"Just having a hard time adjusting to being home, I guess."

"That's very normal. Many veterans feel that way." She places her hand on my thigh, circling her fingers along the fiber of my shorts.

"Yeah." She's probably looking for real answers here. She wants me to tell her things. Things I can't face. I'd rather talk about the sex we had last night than to tell her about a single second of being overseas.

As if she can read my mind, she brings it up. "About last night. I thought…"

I cut in, "About that. I'm sorry. I should have never crossed that line with you. You're my buddy." Fuck, why would I say buddy? Is she going to assume I mean fuck buddy?

"Oh," she answers in a soft tone.

Shit. "I didn't mean it like that, Lizzy."

"No, it's ok. I get it." But, she doesn't get it. She doesn't truly understand where my head's at.

And I'm too chicken shit to say a word.

"You don't get it, Liz. Come here." I open my arms to her, and she snuggles in beside me. This is so perfect, fuck.

I shake my head. "When I was overseas, it was a lot of waiting for action. Actually, it was a lot of hoping and praying I'd get to use my gun and kill someone."

"Oh," she whispers, and I hope I haven't scared her off.

"We train and train for action and for the first year, I saw none. We all grew restless. The sun was so hot. It was so damn miserable over there."

"I'm sorry," she says with sincerity.

I kiss the top of her head, a habit I could get used to. "I missed you a lot."

She leans back into my arms, and I kiss the top of her head again. I need to stop, but her hair smells so good. It's a smell I'd never tire of, like juniper berries. It brings me back to when we were younger and I could always tell when she was near by the smell of juniper berries.

"I missed you too," she says with a smile. She's so damn cute. Like really fucking cute.

I squeeze her, never wanting to let her go, but knowing damn well I should. "What about you? What were you doing while I was off defending the country?"

She taps a finger to her plump bottom lip. "Not much. School. I dated a few guys."

I clench my teeth listening to her talk about other men. "Oh," is all I offer up.

"Nobody that great."

"I'm sorry." Not really. I'm glad she's not together with anyone. I really like her, and my heart crashes in my chest with the thoughts of never having her.

"Meh, I'm happier now," she says with a shrug.

"Are you?"

"Yeah." She nuzzles in deeper to my side, and I kiss the top of her head, again. This time leaving my lips in her wild hair a bit longer than necessary. "Are you?" she asks.

"Right now, I am."

"Did you finally get to see some action?"

She wants to know if I've killed anyone. Unlike my younger brothers, who just came right out and asked, she may not really want to know the answer.

"Yeah, I saw a lot. Action I wish I could erase."

"Did you," she pauses, "kill anyone?"

I raise my hand to my face, pinching the bridge of my nose before answering, "A few."

"Oh. Was it hard?"

I chuckle for a second. "Killing or dealing with it?"

"Both, I suppose."

"No," I clip out. I want to tell her how I killed the men I did only because it was either them or me. Them or the men I called friends. But I remain quiet.

"I'm proud of you, Ryan." She wraps her arms around my waist, her head still on my chest. "I really am. I don't think I could handle it."

"Who says I am?"

"You got a Purple Heart Medal, right? Don't they only give those out to injured soldiers?"

"Yeah, I guess."

She studies me, her eyes asking all the questions she won't say aloud. She drags her hand along my face and leans up to plant her lips on mine.

I need to push her away, but the touch of her lips is something I can't deny myself anymore. God, the things I want to do to her. One more night. Please.

Breaking the kiss, I stare into her heated eyes. Fuck, I'm so turned on. She repositions, straddling me, as she leans in for another kiss. I let her. I think I might always let her. I'm a moron.

She grinds her hot heat against my growing cock, and it's getting harder and harder to deny her. I grip her ass in my hands, helping her along. "I need to taste you, Lizzy." One taste.

"You can do whatever you want to me."

I smooth her tresses back and claim her lips again. Her mouth tastes like heaven. I can only imagine what the rest of her will taste like. I'm dying to find out.

Lying her on her back on the couch, I move my hands to her shorts and slip them off with ease. She arches, and I nearly lose it. Her yellow, lace panties cover her sweet pussy from me, and I tug at them and lower them down her long, silky legs. She's a kaleidoscope of beauty, with varying lights and shapes all phasing together to turn her into a work of art.

I spread her legs, and my cock hardens. "Take your shirt and bra off for me," I command.

She complies, and the sight of her full tits has me eager and ready to get inside her again.

I lower my head, starting with her tits, licking and sucking each nipple into my mouth. My hands grip her hips as I work her body to new heights.

Making my way south down her body, I throw each leg over my shoulders. Her pussy greets me as I lower into her. Licking along her skin, her wetness coating my tongue, I bury my face between her legs.

"Oh God, Ryan." Her fingers pull hair, and I don't care if I go bald.

I clasp her clit between my lips, begging for more, as my heart beat slams around in my chest. My body is on fire, a deep burning that'll never go out.

I fuck her pussy with my tongue. I fuck her whole pussy with my face, as she grinds over and over against me. With one hand running all the way up her stomach and the other reaching around her back, I turn her almost sideways as I go deeper and deeper. My cock throbs at the sounds she makes. My body comes alive with the way she moves. Fuck, this girl is perfect for me. I just wish I was perfect for her.

∼

CHAPTER 12

LIZARD

 Love is friendship set on fire.

I'm so close. I am *so* close. Close to coming. Close to giving this man my heart. Close to, hell, maybe even loving him.

I've never felt anything like this before, and it scares me.

I'm on the precipice of love and like. Or maybe it's lust. Either way, I've got it bad for him.

Every touch brings me closer to the edge of my orgasm. I push myself harder against his face, tugging his hair in the process. "Fuck, Ryan," I scream.

My body crashes and burns. Falls and takes flight. Dies a tiny death and is reborn. The best fucking orgasm I've ever had ripples through my body, propelling me into a new sense of feeling.

A feeling I didn't know was possible.

My orgasm doesn't stop and neither does Ryan. They both have other things in store for me as my body climbs and plummets all at once.

He lifts me from the couch, stalks to his bedroom, and tosses me on the bed. When he flips me over and smacks my ass, I go insane with desire.

"I'm nowhere near done with your sweet pussy yet," he husks out while rolling a condom down his thick cock.

I so want this. I want everything he has to offer.

He grips my hips, lining me up with him. I wait for it with anticipation, knowing he works my body so good. He enters me, and my ravenous body kicks into high gear. Skin slapping, hair pulling, teeth grinding, and loud cursing come together in a sexual potpourri of magic and lust. A primal lust, one filled with two souls who have found each other in the insanity of this world.

I think a relationship can work. I'm willing to try. Hell, if I can get this type of animalistic fucking most nights of the week, I'll do all the work.

He leans close to my ear, whispering, "Your pussy is so damn tight, little girl. It owns me."

My chest explodes at his words, and tingles of the first wave of another orgasm light up my surface.

I can't form any words to respond, instead I keep taking his thrusts and as he reaches around to toy with my clit. I lose every bit of control and come hard.

He palms my breasts, his body still rocking into me from behind. "Fuck, you're perfect."

In one fluid motion, he pulls out, flipping me over as he rips off the condom and comes all over my stomach. I rub it over my nipples as he groans out more of his release. "God, you're sexy as fuck," he says as his eyes roam over my body.

After we've calmed down, I hop into the shower to clean myself. When I return, Ryan is sprawled out, sleeping. Quietly, I nestle into his body and fall asleep.

Halfway through the night, I awake to Ryan sitting in a chair beside the bed, in the dim light. His chest rises and falls, and his thumb brushes over his jaw as he studies me through his thick eyelashes. I wrestle with the sheets a tad as I move my body, facing him. "What are you doing?"

"Memorizing you."

My chest warms. "Come back to bed," I say, reaching out my hand to him.

He crawls in beside me, wrapping his arms around me, spooning up behind me. We fall asleep, and I couldn't be happier.

The next morning as birds chirp just outside the window, I stretch my body, taking a bit longer to wake up.

Ryan isn't in bed, and I grab one of his old t-shirts to wear. I traipse down the hallway in search of him.

"What are you doing?" I ask, when I spot him in the living room, pacing from the leather couch to the far wall.

Startled, he drops the spiral notebook from his hand. With a grin, he says, "Nothing, just scouting my living room."

"Oh, is the enemy present here?"

He laughs. "Maybe soon."

I move toward him, wrapping my arms around his neck. With a light peck to his cheek, I smile. "You're safe with me. I'll protect you."

He grabs me, leaning me over a bit, and plants a big kiss on my lips. After breaking the kiss, he whispers, "I might hold you to that one day."

Our eyes lock, and heat sizzles between us. My heart bangs. My pulse quickens. "I hope so," I whisper.

He kisses me again, deeper this time. My legs go weak all the way down to my toes.

Passion streams through us. He must feel this too. It can't be just me.

He sets me upright, and gives me that smile.

"Get dressed." He slaps my ass, scooting me off in the direction of the bedroom.

"Why?"

"We're going to have family day at the Wagner's. Oh, it's tons of fun. You remember growing up coming to a few, right?"

I scratch my head. "Yeah, I'm busy today."

"No, don't make me go alone." He chases after me as I rush off down the hall.

I run into the bedroom. "Ryan, no don't make me go." I'm too slow because he picks me up, hauling me over his shoulder.

"If I have to go, so do you," he says, flinging me onto the bed.

"That's not fair." I laugh, lifting my foot to his chest to keep him back.

He grabs my ankle, and pulls me closer to him where he stands at the foot of the bed. "Don't make me go alone, Lizard. I need you."

Needs me. Be still my heart, how could I ever say no.

∼

CHAPTER 13

CRYIN'

> The truth may be out there, but the lies are inside your head.

A few hours later, Lizzy and I sit together on my parent's sea-green sofa listening to Lance tell us about his latest trip to Hawaii.

"This wave had to be about twenty feet easily, bro." He brushes back his sandy blond hair.

I want to shout to everyone here how Lizzy and I are a couple. I want everyone to know how I feel about her.

But, we aren't a couple. As much as I want it, I could never do that to her.

She squeezes my thigh as we continue to listen to Lance. My mother cooks in the kitchen, occasionally calling out to add her tidbits of the family vacation to the North Shore where Lance surfed in a competition.

After awhile, she peeks her blonde head around the corner. "Ryan, come here, please." The formality of her tone isn't a good sign.

I raise a brow to Lizzy before getting up. "Sure thing." I turn to Lizzy. "I'll be right back."

Lizzy practically grew up here as well, so leaving her alone with my brothers isn't a scary ordeal for her. She fits right in with the craziness.

My mother walks past the kitchen and into my father's office. This has always been his office of solitude. The one place we never could enter growing up. Even now, I feel odd being in here.

When my mother shuts the door, I know something is up. Did they find out about Lizzy and I?

"Is everything ok, Ryan?" my father asks, sitting behind his large oak desk.

My mother takes a seat on the small black, leather couch along the far wall.

"Yeah, sure. What's up?" I stand at attention, waiting for my father to say what he has to say.

"I received this from the VA hospital. I guess it was put in our mailbox by mistake." He holds up a few sheets of white paper, and my heart races.

"So, you read it?" I snatch the papers from his hand.

"Ryan, we're just worried," my mother says.

I thumb through the results of my CAT-SCAN. "Everything's fine."

"You would tell us if there is anything seriously wrong with you, right, son?" My father rises from his chair.

I fold the papers up, stuffing them into the pocket of my jeans. "Yeah, of course. It's all precautionary."

"Precautionary," my father repeats.

It's hot in here. Am I suffocating?

My mother rises as well, bringing me in for a hug. "We love you so much."

"Mom, stop. Listen, guys, I'm fine. As healthy as a horse." I smile wide, leaving the stuffiness from the office behind as I rejoin Lizzy and the others.

As healthy as a horse.

Yeah, if the horse had been danger close to an IED explosion.

A million purple hearts could never erase what's lying in store for me.

∽

A few hours later, after we've eaten and spent ample time with the family, I take Lizzy outside to sit on the back deck over the water.

The lake has dried up some since I left, but it's still large enough to ride the jet skis on during the weekend.

We sit, dangling our feet over the edge. The sun sets in the west, painting the sky, as we splash our toes in the water.

"So," Lizzy begins.

"So," I repeat.

It's awkward.

There's so many things I want to tell her. Last night was great, something I'll always cherish. But, we need to move on. One night of enchantment, and now it's time to be real with her. This will never work.

For one split second I thought it would. After being cornered in my parent's office, reality set in.

"You're being weird. Should we talk about this?" She takes a deep breath, and so do I.

"Yeah. Lizzy, I think you're great." Already I'm botching this mission before it's begun.

"Oh no." She covers her face, then drops her hands. "Don't do this to me. If you want to pretend like it never happened that's fine with me. We can go back to being friends."

Her hair drifts around her face from the wind. She's stunning. I'm so lucky to even get to lay eyes on her.

"It's not that. I don't think I could ever pretend it didn't happen." I swallow hard. "I just think you deserve better."

Her eyes cut to me. "Don't give me that line of baloney."

I laugh at her word choice. Then back to all seriousness, I continue, "I'm not the same guy I used to be. What if it didn't work out? I don't want to lose you."

"Well, me either. What I went through with my parent's divorce devastated me."

"Yeah, I remember. I don't want us to ever go through anything like that." I wrap an arm around her shoulder. "I don't ever want to put you through that."

"I get it. Yeah, it sucked coming from a broken home. But, look at your parents. Still in love after all these years." Her eyes meet mine. "Look at my sister Alice. And, my friend Kayla. She met a great guy. They're all happy."

I kiss the top of her head. An action I am growing fond of. An action I'll miss. "I can't make you happy. The war fucked my head up pretty bad."

She sits up, my arm dropping in the process. "What do you mean?"

I don't want to tell her. The ugliness of war is not a place for her. She doesn't need to know. "It's fine. I'm just not the same guy anymore."

"I like the guy you are now." She rubs her hand down my chest, her fingers reaching underneath the hem.

"I just don't think I can do this anymore."

"Do what?" she asks. She knows. I see it on her face. It's fucking killing me.

"Us."

Her fingers feel like voodoo. I twist my fingers in her hair, bringing her lips to me and kiss her with everything I have. Everything I wish I could give her.

I'll do anything for this girl, except be with her.

~

CHAPTER 14

LIZARD

> Walking with a friend in the dark is better than walking alone in the light.

Why is heaven sometimes hell? Because that's what this feels like. Happiness just out of reach. Bliss mixed with all the worries of what if. If he would only try, he would see how right this is. His kiss grows deeper, and I run my fingers under the ridge of his waistband, letting my touch speak the things I can't say. He breaks the kiss and lingers for a moment.

"Let me take you home," he says.

※

"I don't get it," Lexi says, grabbing two wine glasses from the shelf.

"Me either." I sit on a stool in our kitchen, and Lexi pours a white, bubbly number into our empty stem glasses.

"Men." She clinks her glass with mine, downing about half the wine in one chug.

"Tell me about it."

After Ryan said he didn't want to be with me, I found Lexi and told her everything.

"Men suck. They really do. They never tell you how they're feeling."

I sip my wine, letting the bubbles fizz on my tongue before swallowing. "I think they're incapable of feeling anything."

"True that." She clinks her glass with mine again, finishing off the rest of her wine.

After a few more glasses and a lot more chatter, we move into the living room.

"I think I've given up on men," Lexi states as she sips more wine.

We're on our second bottle now, and my mind is so occupied with Ryan, I can't focus.

"Why?" I ask.

"They just don't get it. Look at you for example. You and this guy, Ryan, are perfect for one another from what you tell me."

"Yeah." If only Ryan thought so.

"And yet, he won't commit. I don't get it. What are men so afraid of?"

"I don't know," I murmur. She rambles on as I listen to her, contemplating on where to go from here.

No, fuck this. I know he wants me.

I jump from the couch, almost spilling my wine.

"Where are you going?"

"I'm calling him. This is bullshit," I rant.

I march into the kitchen, searching for my phone in the piles of mail and women's magazines strewn all over the counter. "Where are you?" I call out to my phone.

"Whoa, calm down." Lexi says, coming up behind me.

"No," I declare with one finger pointed in the air. Maybe I'm a bit drunk, but I don't care. I didn't imagine the way he spoke to me, kissed me, touched me. He wants me. And whatever stupid reason he thinks he has, well, I'm not going down without a fight. "I need to talk to him."

"Ok, good luck. I'm off to bed." Lexi stumbles down the hallway to her room.

I find my phone. Hallelujah. With blurry vision, I press his name and hit send. And, I wait.

It isn't too late, and on the third ring he answers.

"Ryan," I say after his groggy hello.

"Hey, you. What's wrong?"

"Um, well, nothing. I just want to see you. Can you come over please?"

"Yeah, I'm on my way," he whispers.

We hang up, and already my mind races with what I want to say to him when he gets here.

I pace my living room. More like stumble around.

I'm not that drunk. I'm more buzzed. A good tingly tipsy feeling that radiates through my blood giving me courage.

A knock at my door throws me off balance.

Do not jump his bones I repeat as I walk to the door. Do not jump his bones.

I throw the door open, and fuck, I want to jump his bones.

He stands there, hands in the pockets of his jeans, with his head hanging low. He gazes at me through his thick, dark lashes, and I'm so fucked.

I've always compared other guys I've dated to Ryan. And, maybe that's why things never worked out. No one could ever live up to the real deal.

Ryan, in all his glory, stands on my doorstep, offering his friendship, and all I want to do is jump his bones.

I'm a bad friend. I should say something.

"Fuck this," Ryan says, slamming the door shut as he charges through it, lifting me in his strong arms.

Carrying me over to the couch, he sits with me straddling his lap. Our lips fuse together, and his tongue seeks mine. His hands trail up my neck, fingers rifling through my hair. It's soft and gentle but holds such power in every stroke.

I break the kiss, my head spinning. "I can't stop thinking about you. I know you said you don't see a future between us, but I think you're wrong."

His thumbs glide down my cheek, running over my bottom lip. "I adore you, Elizabeth." His mouth draws me in slowly, a deep, long kiss, scorching my insides.

I grind against him while my hands race down his chest, slipping underneath the waistband of his denim, searching for him.

He picks me up, carrying me back to my bedroom and quietly shuts the door. My feet touch the soft carpet of the floor.

"I want to own these pretty lips of yours." His deep, raw voice sends a shockwave through my system. He pushes on my shoulder, unzipping his jeans, and I kneel before him.

My hands on his thighs, his big cock right in front of me, I take the tip deep in my mouth. His head hits the door, his eyes closing, as he moans out my name.

I use my hands to hold him steady, and take him in as deep as I can.

CHAPTER 15

CRYIN'

 Courage is endurance for one moment more.

Oh fuck, she sucks my cock like a hoover. Best damn blow job I've ever had is Lizzy's sweet lips sucking me off.

She's a master at it. A pro. I don't know which way is up or down right now.

My knees feel heavy, and all I want to do is slam my dick deep down her throat. I want to come, but I need to fuck her first.

I tug her hair, my cock slipping from her hungry mouth. She glances up at me, her big browns questioning.

"Get on the bed, beautiful."

She does as I say, and I follow her. Our clothes come off with every step. My body aches with a powerful need only she will be able to satisfy.

It's always been her. Even before I ever knew I wanted her. Back in school, I hated seeing her out with guys.

I always thought it was because I wanted to protect her, but now I know it was pure jealousy.

Every day while overseas I thought about her. Wondering

where she was. Wondering if she thought about me. Wondering if she was happy.

I start with her foot, kissing my way up her leg. Her skin is silky smooth. Her smile widens as I get closer to her pussy.

Pushing her legs apart, I swipe my tongue along her soaked heat. My body is all kinds of on fire. I can't take much more of her. She's everything.

I swipe my tongue again, loving the sounds coming from her mouth. I want more. My body can't survive this.

I continue sucking and biting as she claws at my skin. Her nails dig deep as I lick and kiss her tender flesh.

She loves this. Hell, she might even love me. And, who knows I might even love her. I've known her my whole life, and even in my darkest times overseas, she never left me.

Even if just to lay my eyes on her one more time.

I move my tongue up her skin, passing every sweet spot I love about her tight figure. I settle at her tits, her nipples peaking, to suck and bite. Her skin heats under my touch.

I was an idiot to think I could ever stop wanting her the way I do. When she called me tonight, I was already halfway to my truck by the time she asked me to come over. My mind was already fantasizing this exact scenario before I even stepped foot into her place.

"You can do whatever you want to me, Ryan," she moans, and her voice eggs me on more.

My dick is like iron and steel, there's no stopping it.

Funny thing is, I can picture a future with her. Maybe it won't be so bad. Maybe the doctors are wrong. Maybe I can have everything the way I want it.

I flip Lizzy on top of me, so she can ride my cock. I want to watch her all night. Watch her as she sinks her pussy down on me.

Never forgetting the way, she looks taking me in, her head falling back, hair cascading down to her ass.

But, it's her tits I focus on. They bounce as she grinds.

"Ride my cock faster."

My hands on her hips guide her. She picks up speed, and her body takes all of me. The pleasure in her face says it all.

She wants me as much as I want her.

My body builds, aiming right toward a release I won't be able to control. I stroke her clit and she takes off. Her hands grip onto my chest, her body riding me hard and fast.

"I'm coming," she moans as her body falls over, her lips meeting mine.

I pound off inside her, the condom catching my release.

Our bodies rise and fall in unison, climbing and tumbling together. I've never had sex so good in all my life. I never knew it could be like this.

After I clean up, we lie in bed, cuddled together.

"I want to be with you," she whispers into my chest.

"I want this too, Lizzy." And I do. More than anything.

Kissing the top of her head, I imagine a life with her. How sweet it will be.

"Are you happy with your life?" I ask her.

"I'm happier now."

"Yeah, but you're happy being a physical therapist?"

She pauses for a moment, her fingers tracing patterns against my chest. "Yeah, I was thinking of going to nursing school. What about you?"

I take a deep breath and let it out slowly. "My dad keeps asking me when I'm going to sign up for classes. I just don't know."

"Well, what's holding you back?"

"I don't want to keep anything from you," I whisper.

She props up on her elbow. "Then don't."

I gaze up to the popcorn ceiling. "When I was overseas, we

were invading this town. Everything was going according to plan. We were almost through when our unit went under attack."

"Were you scared?"

"Yes and no. We were finally getting some action, and I was ready to fight. I felt like we were getting the short end of the stick. Everyone was seeing action but us. We were being sent on stupid missions, and I wanted more. The government spends a lot of money training us, and I felt like we weren't being utilized properly."

"I think I'd be terrified."

"It's different when it's happening. Your training kicks in. You focus on your objective and get it done."

"Oh," she whispers.

"When we went under attack, we were far enough out of the city. Another Humvee blew a gasket. It all went to shit after that."

"But you're safe now." She kisses my chest.

"Yeah, I know. But there's more." I pause. "I really thought I'd never come home. I thought we were all sitting ducks, and I wasn't sure I'd survive."

"You did survive."

I clam up, not wanting to go deeper into anything tonight. I don't want to worry her when even the doctors don't know the extent of the effects of the IED explosion or how bad it is.

"I did survive." And, I'm thankful for that. I'm thankful to hold her in my arms.

She falls asleep as I listen to her breathing. Hours later, after my mind has calmed from memories of my time overseas, I close my eyes and endure a dreamless sleep.

∼

In the morning, I awake to my phone ringing in the pocket of my jeans. Where are my jeans?

I examine the floor, spotting them near the door.

Answering, I'm met with my younger brother, Lance's, voice on the other end.

"We need your truck and help. Can you come to Mom and Dad's?"

"Yeah, I'm on my way," I say as Lizzy stirs in the bed.

I hang up, tossing my phone on her white, wooden nightstand.

She opens her eyes, groggy and still half-asleep. "Morning," she says, yawning.

"Want to come to my parent's house with me? I've been summoned for my truck, so I'm sure heavy lifting is probably involved."

She stretches her body against her soft, red sheets. "Sure, just let me get ready."

We pull up to my parent's house a while later and walk inside.

The place appears calm, and I wonder why I was called. My mother steps into the front room as we close the door.

"Back here. We need your help." She keeps walking and talking as we follow. "The shipment for new surfboards came, and they delivered it here instead of at the shop."

I scrub a hand down my face. "You want to load them up in my truck, sure."

I grab Lizzy's hand and kiss it in front of my mother and tell her I'll be right back. My mother's eyes light up. I'm sure a part of her always wanted us together.

I walk into the back room where my father and brothers are hovered over roughly thirty boards.

The sun streams in through the large open windows, casting a hot glow against each board. Lizzy and my mother hang back in the kitchen as I step further into the room.

"Looks like a mess," I say to them, laughing. Briefly, I feel like maybe my life isn't.

∽

CHAPTER 16

LIZARD

 One day love and friendship met.

Mrs. Wagner's eyes went wide when Ryan kissed my hand, a fact not lost on me. We sit together at the old wooden table with white legs. A table I've come to know over the years of coming here. This place was my haven when my parents split up. Even before, when there was nothing but fighting, I would escape to Ryan's house, begging for him to save me from the madness of my own life.

My mother was a mess, and my father was an asshole. Even still to this day I don't talk to him much. He tried for a while, buying Alice and I anything we wanted, whenever we spent time with him. But, after a while he came around less and less. And, as we grew older we never wanted to see him much either.

My mother was a non-existent mother, crying herself to sleep most nights and working her life away during the days. I don't fault her for any of it. I love and respect her, but I know she didn't have it easy after the divorce.

My father remarried, a girl half his age and not much older

than Alice. My mother never did. She's still alone, but swears she's happier now.

Most times during my teens, it was Ryan's mother I went to for advice. I think she always knew I had a thing for Ryan growing up, but I would never admit that to her.

"Want some coffee?" she asks.

"Sure."

"I'll put a pot on. They'll probably be awhile," she says, grabbing the pot and running it under the faucet to fill it with water. I trace my fingers across the table scarred with memories. I feel weird, like she sees me as a daughter, so technically, this is incest. Ugh. Is that how she sees us?

Once the coffee is made and she offers me a cup, she sits down and we continue our idle chatter until she finally asks about him.

"Are you in love with my son?"

I nearly choke on my coffee. I didn't expect that question. Are you sleeping with him? Are you dating him? Anything except love.

As much as I want to say yes, we've only reconnected recently. "I could love him."

She pats my hand with hers. "I always knew you were the woman for him." Oh, thank god. "And, I couldn't be happier. He's a good man."

"Yeah," I say, taking a sip of my hot coffee.

A frown tugs at her lips. "I'm worried about him."

I set my cup down. "Why?"

She glances down to her aging hands. "No reason. I just worry. It's what mothers do."

Her hazel eyes meet mine, and I offer up a smile. "You sure?"

She nods, and we sip our coffee as the boys carry surfboards through the hallway and out of the house. Every so often I catch Ryan staring at me as he passes by the kitchen, and my heart melts.

"Did I ever tell you about the time Ryan first met you?" his mother asks me.

"No. I think we were five, right? Kindergarten?"

"Yes. He came home from school and said he'd met a new friend. A best friend. I asked about his new friend, and he told me about you. He said you were the prettiest girl in the whole class." She smiles. "He said you were going to be best friends forever."

I laugh. "Well, I was kinda hot with the pigtails. But, seriously, he'll always be my best friend."

"Well," she places her hand over mine, again, with a gleam in her eye, "he's very lucky."

I hug her, wrapping my arms around her petite frame. "I just remember him being the only boy in class who was nice to me."

"Ryan's always been a sweetheart. He used to help me cook while his brothers were out back fighting or Lord knows what...Ryan was always here with me."

I lean back, resuming my seat across from her. "Can I ask why he joined the military? In high school, he was always so gung ho about it."

"It was the commercial."

"Commercial?" I shake my head in confusion.

"You know the one. With the man climbing up the volcano, through the lava, and he slays the dragon at the top."

I laugh. "What are you talking about? I've never seen that one."

"Coolest commercial ever. I wanted to be a marine so I could kill dragons," Ryan says, sneaking up behind me, wrapping his strong arms around me. He nuzzles his nose into the crook of my neck as I laugh along with them.

I'm happy. And I want this always.

"So, Ryan the dragon slayer...sexy." I giggle.

"Who's a dragon slayer?" Lance asks, walking into the kitchen.

"Ryan is. Did you slay any dragons over in Afghanistan?" Devin asks.

He kisses the top of my head before letting go, standing up to tower over his brothers. "Yeah, big ones."

He grabs Lance, his arms wrapping around his neck, locking

him in place. All three wrestle in the kitchen. Devin lunges toward Ryan, hitting Lance's head in the process.

"Take it outside," his father barks, trying to break them up before they shatter the many glass containers filled with pasta and cereal on the granite countertops.

Ryan winks at me before the three disappear outside.

"You sure you want to date him?" his mother asks me.

I smile, a warm feeling traveling through me. "I'm sure. "

Later, when the sun has disappeared and the night sky is twinkling with stars, Ryan and I sit outside snuggled in the large hammock tied between two royal palms. He holds me close, his fingers twirling through my hair.

"I could get used to this," Ryan says against my ear.

"Me too."

And I could. I used to imagine this scenario all the time in my head. A new beginning to a happily ever after.

CHAPTER 17

CRYIN'

" Say goodbye to the sun.

The past few weeks with Lizzy have been amazing. We're building toward something. A future I want more than anything.

Fuck the doctors. Fuck the psychiatrist. I won't let this war change me. I'm fine.

I walk into work with a big smile on my face.

"Someone's happy," my mother says as I walk behind the old converted surfboard counter where the register sits.

"Yeah, I guess I am."

"Is it a certain blonde making you feel this way?" she asks, knowingly.

"Yes, Mom, you always make me happy." I kiss her cheek, and she smiles.

"Not me, silly. I meant Lizzy."

I knew what she meant. And, Lizzy makes me extremely happy. "Yeah, her too."

My mother beams as I get to work.

It's summertime here in Miami, and the onslaught of locals we get in the store today is overwhelming.

By the end of the day, my head is throbbing. A throb so bad, I pop a few pills before I head out to meet Lizzy at the beach for an afternoon swim in the ocean.

I grab a new board I've had my eye on and head out to my truck and hop in.

As I walk up to the shore, the hot sand under my feet, I spot her dipping her toes in the ocean.

She waves her hand as I step closer.

I set the board down and pick her up, spinning her around as I plant my lips on hers. "Ready for another lesson?"

"How about I sit here and just watch."

I kiss her cheek, and grab my board. "Ok, suit yourself," I say, taking off running into the ice-cold water.

The tide isn't too high and the waves break a bit too soon, but, all in all, a good day for surfing. I paddle out. The sun reflects off the sea, casting a few shadows in my vision.

A perfect wave comes at me, and I turn my board and stroke my arms faster. I catch it at the right time and hop to my feet. It's the best feeling in the world, riding a wave. A freeing, relaxing calm washes over me, and I twist and turn my body to stay up.

As soon as the ride is over, I paddle back out for more. I've been riding waves since before I could ride a bike. My father had us out on the ocean at an early age, and it's the one thing that centers me when I'm stressed.

I missed the beach while I was overseas. But, I missed Lizzy more. The men I served with just weren't as funny as her.

I catch another wave and wipeout the second my feet land on the board. The wave crashes over my head, tumbling me along the sandy ocean floor. When I finally resurface, my head aches so badly I can barely see straight.

"You ok, soldier?" Lizzy asks, as I head over to where she lies on a red beach towel. With a book in her hand, and wearing huge sunglasses and a floppy hat, she smiles up at me.

"Yeah, I have a bit of a headache. Want to get some food?"

"Uh, sure. We can hit that pizza diner place."

Ah, Papa Giorno's was a hot spot in our teens. High school kids hung out there every weekend, and I'm sure with the laid-back atmosphere and arcade games in the back, the place is still crawling with young kids.

I follow her closely on her Vespa. My truck is huge compared to her tiny little ride, but it suits her. She's never been a normal girl. Always doing things her way. Like at graduation, she was the only girl in school in black combat boots and shorts under her robe.

She's not a combat boot type of girl, but she wore it she said in "support" of me joining the military. I think she did it more to rebel me joining instead, but I'd never tell her that. She was in enough trouble from the school administrator that day for not dressing "properly".

She's always marched to the beat of her own drummer, and it's one of the things I've always been fascinated by.

In the military being unique was frowned upon. We were just a number, a machine, a weapon for them to use. And I was ok with it. I wanted it. In the military, they say killing is only bad if you don't enjoy it. I heard that the whole time I was there. Kill this person, don't kill that one. Kill that guy, don't kill that one. They all looked the same. It grew harder the longer I was there.

The first man I killed was quick. It shocked me at first, seeing the blood. It took me a second to realize I pulled the trigger, but he had an RPG aimed at my unit.

It got easier after that. It's only wrong if you don't enjoy it. But, sometimes I think it's only wrong if you do.

The things I saw will haunt me for a lifetime, but I don't regret going. I don't regret anything I did. It's funny, if I was here in the US and did the same things, I'd be in jail...maybe even death row. But, war is a different monster.

When the IED explosion happened, I lost two of my friends. Davis saved my life that afternoon. He died shortly after, his body not surviving the blast. But, I survived.

I was discharged immediately, the doctors claiming I wasn't fit to fight, claiming I sustained a brain injury. I was on the first flight back to the states.

They went over everything I could experience for the rest of my life, but it's all guesswork. No doctor can predict the future. The first doctor said I wouldn't survive the flight home. Another talked about losing fine motor skills.

All in all, no doctor knows everything. They're just guessing, like the rest of us.

I park my truck beside her blue bike and hop out.

"I'm starving," she says, removing her black helmet and running her fingers through her long locks.

I open the door for her and take stock of the joint. Yep, I was right...nothing but a bunch of teenagers. We fall into a red, vinyl booth and my stomach grumbles. Taylor Swift, or some other teeny bopper artist, plays from the jukebox in the corner. It's loud and aggravates my already pounding head.

"What do you want?" she asks, grabbing her copy of the menu.

"I'm easy. Go ahead and get your ridiculous, nasty pineapples. I'll pick them off."

When the waitress returns, we place our order and then grab hands across the table.

"Did you want to see a movie tonight? I've been wanting to see that new romantic comedy," Lizzy says.

I roll my eyes. "Ok." Anything for her.

The same group of guys from the other night catches our attention as the server puts our sodas in front of us. Six or seven gangly men stand near a few of the arcade games laughing loudly and busting each other's chops. The place is packed and the constant chatter drowns out the music playing from the jukebox.

Our pizza arrives, and I pick off a few pineapples and take a bite.

"Oh God, not them again," Lizzy

says, jabbing a finger in the direction of the guys making a ruckus.

"Don't worry. I'm sure they learned their lesson." I raise my fingers to my temple and try to massage out the pounding of the migraine coming on.

"Are you ok?"

"Yeah, I'm fine."

The group in the back make fun of a younger teenager, and they're trying my patience. Lizzy senses my agitation and pats my hand with hers. "They're a bunch of jerks."

"Yeah." I finish off my slice and grab another, removing the heinous yellow cubes of fruit.

"You should try a pineapple," Lizzy says, laughing.

"No thanks. It's gross."

She takes a huge bite, grabbing a few of my discarded pineapples and tossing them in her mouth. "Yum, delicious. You should try one."

"You've been trying for years to get me to eat pineapple. I've had it before, I just don't like it." I laugh.

"Ok," she peeks over her shoulder at the jukebox in the back, "I'm going to go put on a song. Save my spot."

She walks away, her long legs carrying her through the restaurant like she owns it. I pop a pineapple in my mouth and immediately regret it. The sour aftermath of it makes me pucker my face, and I grab a sip of my soda as Lizzy puts her money in the machine.

I squint as the sun's rays slam through the restaurant and hide

her image from me. Blinking a few more times, my mind races. Oh no. It's happening. Guess the doctors were right. Fucking IED.
   Not now.

Not here.

Please God. No.

God doesn't listen, and my whole world crashes.

CHAPTER 18

LIZARD

" Sometimes being a true friend is not enough.

I know just the song for Ryan. The jukebox has to have Backstreet Boys. I laugh and lower my finger along the glass as I try to read each title.

The horrible guys from the back move closer as I pretend not to notice. I lean over the machine as one of them comes up behind me.

"Need help? Don't play something stupid," a smelly man says. It's the same one whose finger was twisted by Ryan. His toxic fumes of body odor and cigarettes waft through my nose. I ignore him, but he doesn't stop. His friends have gathered around, and I quickly choose any song as they box me in.

The place is overrun by school kids, and no one even pays attention to us in the back.

"Can I go to my seat?" I push on the main guy's chest.

"We just want to talk to you a little," another redheaded man says.

"Well, I don't really want to talk to you." I try to push past, but these guy's tower over me. I laugh a little, knowing nothing too bad can happen in such a public place.

"I have my own man to talk to, thanks."

"Who that idiot over there?" A blond guy points in the direction of Ryan, and I glance over to him.

What is he doing?

I stand on tiptoes to gain a better view of Ryan knocking over a few things on the table as he tries to stand up. He bumps right into the waitress carrying a large tray of drinks and everything crashes to the floor.

Something's not right.

"Let me through." I push on the man's arm.

"Lizzy," Ryan calls as he stumbles, falling to his knees on the broken glass on the floor.

The guys cornering me laugh. "Look at that fucking moron. That's your boyfriend?"

Something's wrong.

With my nails, I dig into the tallest man's arm as hard as I can.

"Fucking bitch," he says, stepping a little to the side.

"You need to get back to that retarded boyfriend of yours," another guy says. I slam my foot into his shin and rush over to Ryan's side.

"Are you okay?" the waitress asks as she picks up shards of broken glass.

Ryan's on his hands and knees, almost crawling through the glass.

I crouch down, placing my hands on his shoulders. "What's going on, Ryan?"

"I can't see," he whispers. "I can't see anything."

My heart races. "What do you mean?"

"I can't see anything."

I wave my hand in front of his face, noticing the far off look in his eyes. They don't focus on me, and I need to get him out of here. "Ok, listen to me. We're leaving."

I stand up, helping him to his feet.

"Do you need help?" the waitress asks, motioning to another server.

The whole restaurant has gone quiet, I'm not even sure if the music's still playing from the speakers.

My heart slams in my chest. "No, I just need to get him to the hospital."

"Should I call 911," says a man rushing over in a suit and tie.

"No, I'll take him." I grab Ryan's arm, linking mine in his to guide him out. Crowds of people have gathered around, but in my panic their voices aren't registering. I walk with him out the glass doors, and his foot gets caught in the threshold, tripping him a bit. "Lizzy, please help me."

"I'm sorry. I'm trying." Tears sting my eyes as I search for his truck in the lot, walking slowly as to not let him trip on anything else. "Where are your keys?" I ask.

"Left pocket." He digs for them, holding them in his fingers and out away from me.

I help him into the passenger side of the truck and bring my hand to his face. "I'm taking you to the hospital."

My heart breaks when I see the expression on his face. "I've never been so scared in all my life," he whispers.

"We'll get this figured out." I shut his door and rush to the other side.

Racing down the street on my way to Mount Sinai Hospital, my mind is unable to catch up to the events happening. What the hell is going on?

The car is silent, and I'm not sure what to even say. I drive through the traffic of the late afternoon, hoping everything will be fine.

"Are you ok?" Lame question I know, but he's not the only one afraid.

"All I see are shadows. Like I know when you turn the car, or when you are driving away from the sun, but that's it. I'm kind of freaking out here."

"I know. We're almost there," I reassure him. "They'll get you all fixed up soon. I'll call your family when we get there."

He leans his head back into the seat and closes his eyes. My fingers tremble as I pull into the emergency room parking lot.

After signing him in and calling his parents, the nurses call for him. "Wait for my parents," he says.

My heart cracks a bit. I want to be in there with him, finding out what's going on.

Staying in the waiting room is torture. Like pure hell not knowing what's happening. His parent's burst through the doors and spot me sitting in the back of the large room.

"What's happening? Where is he?" his mother asks.

"He's with the doctor now."

"What exactly happened?" Mr. Wagner asks.

I tell the story to his parents and younger brother, Lance, and his mother cries.

"I knew something wasn't right." She sobs into her husband's chest.

"Calm down, Barb. We don't know anything yet."

I pace the room, needing to calm my overactive nerves.

And then, the doctor walks in.

CHAPTER 19

CRYIN'

> Keep your head up. God gives his hardest battles to his strongest soldiers.

Blindness. Damage to the optic nerve. These terms rattle around my mind as I sit in the cold room trying to figure out my next course of action.

The door opens, and I lift my head at the sound.

"Oh, my God, Ryan," my mother says, her arms wrapping around me. Her perfume invades my nose in a way I've never noticed before. She softly sobs against my chest as I wrap my arms around her as best I can.

When the doctor left the room, I asked him not to let Lizzy back here. Only my parents. I don't want her to see me this way.

Everyone has a conception of a marine. Of a man. And I didn't want her to see me at my weakest. I'm still in shock, but I always knew it was a possibility from the moment Dr. James mentioned it on my first evaluation.

But, you never think it can happen to you.

And, as much as you prepare, you're never prepared for when it finally happens. The seriousness never hits you until you're sitting at a restaurant, eating pizza, and your sight is stripped away from you.

I'm trying to be strong for my mother. Hearing her cry breaks my heart. My father's large hand pats my back, and the doctor tells them the same thing he told me—Blind. I'm blind.

I still can't wrap my brain around it. What I want to do is just crawl away in a hole and never come back out.

Trying to be strong, and being strong, are two separate things. On the inside, I'm freaking the fuck out. But, I sit, silently, listening to the doctor talk about treatment options and centers for the blind which can help.

Of course, he tells us to make a follow-up appointment with my primary physician, and then tells us we can be on our way.

But, I don't move. I don't want to be on my way. I want the doctor to fix everything. Like when I was sick as a kid and the doctor would make it all better.

He doesn't make it better, though, just sends us on our fucking way.

My father grabs my arm and helps me from the table. "I'll guide you out. We'll have Lance drive your truck home," he says.

My truck. A truck I'll never get to drive again.

"Is Lizzy still out there?"

"She's worried about you. She's not going anywhere until she sees you."

Until she sees me. I wince as small realizations hit me. I'll never see their faces again.

My father does a good job leading me through the hospital, letting me know about every turn, every little thing which could be an obstacle for me.

The doctor gave me something for my head, and it's making me dizzy. I'm disoriented and a light gets brighter as my father tells me we're heading through the waiting room.

"Ryan." Lizzy's voice is far away but getting closer. "Ryan." Her voice sounds in front of me and her breathing is rapid, and already I know she's crying.

I almost lose control.

Heavier footsteps follow her, and I'm guessing it's one of my brothers. Her tiny arms wrap around my midsection, and her hair tickles my nose. I feel weak in her arms. And I want nothing more than for her to go away.

Sure, it's mean, but I'm a man. I should be the one taking care of her. Not the other way around. I would never ask that of her.

My mother relays a shorter version of what the doctor has said, and all I can think about is if people are watching. I don't hear other people, but I feel eyes on me. It makes me uncomfortable.

"Can we get out of here, please," I ask.

My father is on it, helping me out. I halt my steps.

Before, I could still see shadows, varying shades of light, like a fucked-up kaleidoscope distorting the light back at me.

But, as soon as the salty air hits my face, there's nothing. Blackness, and it fucking terrifies me.

My father senses my hesitation, gripping my arm tighter. "It's ok. I've got you. I won't let you fall."

His soft tone calms me, allowing me to continue walking. Lizzy isn't far behind because I can hear her footsteps, and, honestly, I don't know what to say to her.

"You'll be staying the night with us in your old room," my mother says.

"Yeah, anything you need," Lance's voice sounds behind me.

"Thanks," I mumble.

My father helps me in the car, and I reach for the seatbelt as he shuts the door.

I hate this feeling. Everyone feeling sorry for me. It's one of the worst feelings, and all I want is my sight back and Lizzy by my side.

But, she's better than this.

She's better than me.

I'm nothing but a burden now.

As soon as I'm home, my mother and Lance head to my house to gather a few of my things.

Lizzy helps me outside, and we sit on the wooden swing on the back porch.

"I can't believe any of this," she says.

"You and me both, kid."

"We'll get through this. They have operations. They have a lot of things. Your mother and I were talking about it."

"Stop. Just stop." It's killing me I can't see her.

"I'm sorry. I guess you need some time." She shifts her body closer.

"Time? What good will that do? I'll still be a freak."

She cuts in, "Stop. Don't say that."

"It's not only that. Lizzy, you don't need to be taking care of me for the rest of my life." I'm doing the right thing. Even though it hurts, it's the right thing.

"What?" I hear the fear in her tone. "Ryan we're a team. You and me. I'm not walking away from you."

"Goddammit. Will you listen to me? I don't want to be a burden to you. It's bad enough I'll need my parents now."

"I'm not leaving."

I stand up, anger coursing through me. The bench swings and hits the back of my legs, and I stumble a few steps in front of me. I know the railing is close and put out my hands to reach for it, but there's nothing there. Lizzy swoops in, guiding me the last few steps, and I feel the course wood hit my hand.

I shake my head. "You're better than this."

"I'll give you some time, but I'm not going to stop caring about you. You've been my best friend since we were kids. I'm not giving up on you."

"Well, I wish you would." I'm pissed at the world. I'm angry with everyone, more so with myself. "Go," I tell her. "Leave."

I'm not strong enough to handle this.

"I'm going to get your mother to come out here and help you. It's been a horrible day. I'll check on you tomorrow." She kisses my cheek and every part of me screams for me to lift her in my arms and never let her go.

"Don't bother. I'm not some science project for you to take care of. I don't need you," I lie.

"Well, I need you."

"Too bad. Whatever this was is over now. Just leave me alone."

As much as I want her, I need her too. But, it's my own anger stopping me.

She walks away, her tears louder than the explosion which caused all of this.

∼

Two weeks later, and after scans and scans, Dr. James mentioned a few of my options. Surgery, counseling, centers to help me be more independent. But, I want none of it.

I want to throw in the towel. God, I give up.

As I try to dress myself, I throw my shirt against the wall. "Fuck," I scream.

To say I'm not handling this well is an understatement. I'm barely able to keep my shit together. Yes, I knew going blind was a possibility, but I never wanted to believe it.

I ignored the headaches, hoping it was just stress, or the heat.

The past few days, I've barely emerged from my room. I listen to music and growl at everyone who enters through the doors. It's fucking hard, and everyday I want to give up.

A knock at the door sounds, and I hear my father's voice on the other side. "Ryan, I'm coming in."

"Go away," I yell.

He opens the door anyway. Lovely. Come on in, I guess.

I sit on the bed as my father's footsteps near. He sits next to me. "Ryan, I want to talk to you."

"Please save it." I don't want to hear anymore about the centers or surgeries. I just want to be left alone.

"Well, no. You're going to listen to what I have to say. You're my son, and I'm damn proud of you."

"Save it," I scoff, folding my arms across my chest.

"I am. You went off to war and served your country."

"Yeah, a lot of good it did me." I wish he would go away.

"Listen, son, you were handed a shit hand, but at least you came home to us. At least you're here." His voice rises. "The son I raised is a survivor. The *man* I raised is a *fighter*. And, it pains me to see you giving up so easily."

"I don't know what to do."

"We're all here for you. We aren't going to let you fail. I think you should check out the center Dr. James mentioned." His hand lands on my shoulder. "What's that Marine saying? Improvise, Adapt and *Overcome*."

I take a deep breath, exhaling slowly. "I'll think about it."

And I do, for the next week. It's all I think about, until I realize he's right. Life sucks. It sucks hard. It tests and tests you, and you must face the challenges and never give up. I'm no quitter. I'm a marine.

I make my way through the house, counting steps and using directional cues to guide me, into the kitchen.

My other senses have kicked into full gear, with my sense of smell taking over. Most things I smell first, then hear. Even my sense of touch has amplified. I never knew how things felt in my hand until I lost my sight.

The aroma of pancakes wafts through the air. My mother's soft humming lets me know it's her cooking.

"Hey, Mom," I say, finding a stool to sit on.

"Good morning. Did you want to drive down to that center I was telling you about?"

Ah, yes. The Miami Lighthouse for the Blind. They apparently offer it all. Classes on how to take care of yourself and other useful shit I need. Improvise, Adapt and Overcome. I repeat the mantra in my head.

"Yeah, I'm finally ready."

After breakfast, we hop in the car and set off for the center.

I like the days the best. The outside lights and shadows dance across my vision, letting me know there's still a world out there. It's the night that scares me, when the blackness comes. It makes me unsure of myself. Makes me wants to never wake when I lay my head down.

My mother parks the car after a while of driving, and I wait for her to help me into the center.

Walking in, I'm both terrified and excited.

"I'm going to sign you in," my mother says. While she's gone, I listen to all the sounds around me. A waterfall not far away, birds chirping, and a low hum of the air conditioner catch my attention. It gives me a serene feeling, and I smile when a lady's voice calls my name.

She grabs my hand and leads me away from my mother.

"How are you today?" she asks.

I don't really know how to answer. "I guess I'm good."

New things are upon me, but I'm still not sure if I'll ever be ready to accept it all.

∼

CHAPTER 20

LIZARD

> A true friend's silence hurts more than an enemy's rough words.

I haven't seen or heard from Ryan in almost a month. His mother has kept me updated, and all I want to do is be there for him.

But, I'm giving him space, per his mother's request.

I smell cookies, and walk into our quaint kitchen to find Lexi hovered over the oven.

"Hey," I say, propping a hip against the counter. "What are you doing?"

"I'm trying a new recipe Kayla gave me for fudge cookies." She smiles a hopeful smile.

"How's it turning out?"

"Um, not really too good." She cringes as she stirs batter in a stainless-steel bowl.

"Let me try." I step closer and stick my finger in the bowl to grab a dab of fudge. I bring it to my lips and shake my head. "It's not too bad," I lie.

"Thanks." She stops stirring and wipes her hand on a towel. "Any word from Ryan?"

"No. His mom says the doctors are hopeful. He's been going to a center for the blind. They teach him how to do things on his own."

"Oh, that's good." She shakes her head. "Man, I couldn't even imagine what he's going through. Does he talk to you?" She grabs a glass of water as I stare out the window.

"No," I whisper.

"I'm sorry, Liz. I wish I had the right things to say. And, I wish I could make it better for both of you."

"No, it's ok. I feel the same. I just wish there was something I could do."

"I know it's hard. But you have to imagine what he's going through. It's best if you're just there for him no matter what. Don't let him push you away," Lexi says, with a soft smile.

Sight. I've always taken it for granted. Last night, I tried closing my eyes and walking around my apartment. I made it about three steps before my fear took over.

I close my eyes again and turn around.

"What are you doing?" Lexi asks.

"I just want to try." I take a step forward, reaching out for the cabinet in front of me.

Blackness all around; it's harder than it appears. I turn and try to walk toward Lexi, forgetting the whole makeup of our house. I wish I could have memorized it before I tried.

Memorize.

Ryan scouted his place. Ryan mentioned memorizing me. Did he know this was going to happen?

My eyes fly open, and Lexi's still in the same spot. "What happened?" she asks.

"I think Ryan knew this was coming?"

"What? He knew he was going to go blind?"

I nod. "Yeah. Why wouldn't he tell me?" I grab my keys from the counter and rush toward the door.

"Where are you going?" Lexi calls after me.

"I need to talk to him."

"Good. Don't let him push you away."

I won't again. I'm going to make him realize we can be together.

Nerves skate through me as I stand on the doorstep of the Wagner's residence. Everyone is at the surf shop, and only Ryan is home. That worries me, and I wonder if I should knock or just go on in.

I try the knob, and it's open.

I step inside, and sun streams through the open windows. It's bright and cheery, but I feel anything but because Ryan can't see the clear blue sky anymore or the sun's rays on the ocean he loved so much. It's all been taken from him with no warning.

I walk through the foyer and spot Ryan sitting on the couch. He's wearing Bose headphones on his ears, moving to the beat of whatever music he's listening to.

I stop in my tracks. Fuck. My heart breaks. Is the memory of everything ingrained in his mind? Is he scared and hiding it from everyone?

Tears fill my eyes as he taps his thumb on the arm of the leather couch. A heavy weight settles on my chest. I want to rush over to him and hug him. Give him my sight.

"I know you're there, Lizzy," he says, removing his headphones.

"Oh, I didn't mean...I mean..." I'm at a loss for words.

"Listen, I've had a bad day. What are you doing here?" The tone in his voice isn't friendly, and it makes my tears fall harder.

"I just wanted to see how you were doing. I care about you."

"See me?" He throws his arms in the air, facing in the direction I'm standing. "Well, here it is. This is how pathetic I'm doing. Happy?"

"Happy? No, I'm not happy. Ryan, I miss you. I miss us." I move closer and take a seat on the couch beside him.

"Us?" He laughs. "There is no us now."

I grab his hand. "There will always be an us."

"Are you kidding? Look at me. This isn't a life for you." His anger targets me, but I won't back down. "I won't do that to you," he yells.

"No, I get to decide what I want for my life." He's what I want. He's still the same Ryan, whether he can see me or not. Losing his sight, didn't mean he lost me. "I love you," I say, firmly.

"Love?" he scoffs. "You can't save me, Lizzy."

"You don't need saving," I cry out. "This isn't a death sentence." I grab the sides of his face; my lips close to his. "I love you. I always have. You don't need to see me to feel it. Just like I wouldn't need to see you." I drop my forehead to his. "Love looks not with the eyes, but with the mind."

A muscle ticks in his jaw. "Now who's quoting Shakespeare?" He kisses me, rough and punishing. It's as if his life force is begging for me to understand him. And, I do.

He's hurting, and I want to be there to ease the pain. "Let me show you, Ryan," I whisper.

∼

CHAPTER 21

CRYIN'

 Honor is simply the morality of superior men.

I feel her climb on top of me, straddling my lap. I told her she'd always be safe with me. How can I do that now? My hands find their way to her hips, slide up and trace over thin straps and the delicate slope of her collar bone. A sundress. Her scent, fresh and clean, invades my nostrils. She guides my hands down to her full breasts. My thumbs brush over the stiff peaks of her nipples.

"Read my body, Ryan. Tell me what it's saying to you."

"Fuck, Lizzy," I murmur. An image of her beautiful face, plain as day, enters my mind. She's clear in my mind's eye. I squeeze her nipples and she moans.

"Come with me," she says. I hear the desire in her tone and the slight, quick intake of air as she breathes. She's turned on and so am I. Her body leaves me, and she tugs at my hand, guiding me. By the steps it takes, and the small notch on the door frame when I reach out, I know it's my bedroom. I'm not helpless, I know where everything is positioned. Even Lizzy. I can smell her and feel her in front of me. My mind is filling in the rest as if I can see her.

"Take your clothes off and get on the bed," I tell her. "I want to read your body."

Her scent drifts away and a faint squeak from the queen size bed let's me know she obeyed. Five steps and I'm at the edge of the bed. I know it by heart now. Reaching out, I trace my fingers down her curves. She's naked. Fuck. I remove my clothes and climb on the bed.

"Touch me, Ryan," she begs. "Tell me what I'm feeling."

I reach out and touch her small feet, then drift my fingers up her smooth legs, slow and calculating. "When I touch you like this, your legs tremble and your heartbeat picks up."

"Ryan," she whispers. "Don't stop."

My confidence soars, feeling her reaction to me, and I continue running my hands up her leg, past her knees, up to her toned thighs. Lowering my head, I graze my nose along her skin and breathe in. "You smell so good. Like juniper berries."

Her swift intake of air spurs me on and my hands move closer toward her pussy. "Do you feel how wet I am for you?" she asks.

My cock is almost painful with need for her. I grip her thighs, parting them slightly, and run my nose along her sensitive skin. Goosebumps ignite under my tongue when I lick slowly up her inner thigh? She moans, and the sound vibrates in my cock.

"When I lick you here, you moan. I love listening to you moan." My hands explore further, grazing along the hard planes of hips and the soft curves of her waist, listening to her body,

My tongue dips into her bellybutton, and I smile when her hands tug my hair. How could I think I could live without this? Or that she would let me? I'd never fucking turn away from her if it were reversed. A growl leaves me when I cup her soft breasts and run my thumbs over each nipple. She bucks beneath me.

"You're so ready for me. When I touch your tits, you grind your pussy against me." I keep going, my fingers tracing her neck, collarbone, shoulders, and then my thumb rests against her artery. "Your pulse is racing. Are you ready for me?" I ask, hovering my lips over hers. Her pants vibrate against my mouth.

"Yes, please," she begs.

"I want you to ride my cock." I lie back, and she climbs on top of me. She's right. I don't need to see her to know she wants me. I feel every fucking thing.

∼

CHAPTER 22

LIZARD

> " Good friends are like stars. You don't always see them, but you know they're always there.

His hands are all over me, his lips following, and this is my heaven. I know now he is my forever, and I will never leave him.

He pushes into me, his hardness filling me up. I ride him as his hands and fingers explore every inch of my skin.

"Fuck, Lizzy, you feel so good." He rocks into me, sitting up on the bed to get a better grip.

The way we move together is like magic. A magic only shared between two souls in love. My body builds and builds as he gains control, slamming into me harder. I ride him until he flips me over and throws my legs around his back, ramming into me.

It's powerful and raw.

"Ryan, I'm so close," I shout out.

He groans. "I love feeling you. It's so much more. I know your body."

I kiss him, long and slow, as chills race over my skin. It's all fireworks and hot magma as he kisses me. I see stars and comets, even planets align in my vision as I close my eyes and feel everything he gives me.

He's the one man who can turn me into all smiles and butterflies, and he's the one man I will never tire of. I love him.

I push against his dick, my inner walls tightening as my orgasm nears. His fingers toy with my clit.

My orgasm hits me like a volcano, and he growls in my ear. "Oh fuck, Lizzy."

The feel of everything, all the emotions, all the heartache over the past few weeks swirls through me, making my teary eyes close. "Ryan, I love you," I repeat in his ear as he continues his push and pull.

"I love you," he says as he comes deep inside me. His fingers move up my body, landing on my face as he cups my cheeks in his hands. "In the darkness and shadows, you're all I see."

A tear falls as I lean into kiss him. And I grind myself against his body. "I'm not going anywhere, ever," I breathe into his ear.

"Good," he says.

CHAPTER 23

CRYIN'

> I do not fear the valley; for I am the shadow.

It's been six months since I went blind. And, it has gotten much easier. When it first happened, I didn't want anyone's help. I wanted to hole myself away forever and never come out.

It wasn't until I actually sat down and talked with my dad and doctors that I felt better. They're hopeful that one day I will get my sight back, but for now I just deal with the day-to-day of being blind.

I finally moved out of my parent's house and back into the bungalow with Lizzy. It's been challenging, but she really is the greatest woman I've ever known.

The Lighthouse Center for the Blind has helped a lot. It's one of the reasons I was able to move out on my own.

They've taught me many things on my road to independence.

"You almost ready?" Lizzy yells from across the hallway.

"Yeah." I finish putting on my shoes and head out of our master bedroom.

She's moved to the kitchen and rattles around in the cabinets. I move up behind her, wrapping my arms around her.

"Hey there," she says, turning around. "You look great."

"I'm a little nervous." I haven't been out in public too much. Maybe it's fear of the unknown, maybe it's something else. Either way, tonight is a huge milestone for us.

"You'll be fine. I'll be by your side, always." She kisses my lips, and my unsteady heart calms.

An hour later, we enter a bar. The smell of cigarettes and alcohol invade me as Lizzy helps me to find a seat.

There's a lot of chatter, and the strobe lights dance in my vision.

"Hey there, you two," my mother says.

A hand pats my shoulder. "Good to see you, son," my father says.

The cacophony of voices and clatter of bar glassware grows louder until I hear my brother's voice. It's directed in front of me, and I know he's onstage.

"I'd like to welcome everyone here tonight," he says, his voice amplified by a microphone. The bar quiets down. "This set is dedicated to someone special joining us here tonight. My brother, Ryan, is here. He's a RECON marine who was injured overseas, and I'm so happy he's here tonight. I love you, bro."

I smile as the soft music of guitars and drums starts.

It's a sad song, but Devin's voice, raw and gritty, booms through the microphone. I never knew he could sing like this.

The song picks up, and the energy around me speeds up. Everyone is clapping and cheering along to the chorus of the song, and I even begin tapping my foot along to the beat.

"He's great, isn't he?" Lizzy asks.

"Yeah, he really is. Thank you for bringing me tonight."

"It means a lot to Devin for you to be here." She kisses my cheek.

We continue listening to song after song, and I'm amazed by how well Devin's band plays.

He really could be the next big thing. His music is better than what plays on the radio, and I clap along with the crowd when he finishes.

"I'm glad you could come," Devin says a while after their set has finished.

"Wouldn't have missed it for anything."

A slow song plays overhead, and Lizzy grabs my hand. "Dance with me."

I'm hesitant at first, but I trust her more than anything, so I allow her to lead me on the floor. I pull her close, her body flush against mine.

The smell of her hair, the touch of her skin is perfect. We move to the soft rhythm and I pull her even closer, her hands gripping me tighter. "I love you," I say, as I kiss the top of her head.

"I love you, too."

I lean in close to her ear, kissing her skin quickly before saying, "Love looks not with the eyes, but with the mind. And therefore, is winged Cupid painted blind."

"You know how much I love when you quote Shakespeare to me," she says.

It's true what they say, when you love someone so much, you are in tune with their feelings. I wouldn't change any of my past decisions that have led me here today.

Maybe if I hadn't joined the war, things would have been otherwise. And not always for the better. Life is a crapshoot, and you never know the hand you'll be dealt until it happens and you're left dealing with it all.

You can give up and never try to handle the situation, like I wanted to do, or, you can face it head on.

You'd be amazed at the things I can do all by myself now. I'm learning braille and can function by myself at home.

I can cook, clean, do laundry, dress myself. I've even been to the beach and into the water. My father has been working with me to surf, and although I haven't successfully ridden a wave, I am getting better.

Everyday is a new set of challenges, but with Lizzy by my side I know I can face anything life has in store for me.

EPILOGUE

LIZZY

The night is blooming with possibilities. Ryan swims in the ocean, catching a wave before the sun has cast its last rays on the day.

You'd be surprised how well he handles being blind. Most people would never guess he's blind with how well he maneuvers around.

After he swims on shore, I call to him to let him know where I am.

"Hey," he says, grabbing me around the waist.

"You're all wet." I laugh.

He plops down on the large towel, and I adjust my telescope to gaze up into the sky.

"Anything interesting?"

"No, not really." I focus on a cluster of stars as Ryan gets up and walks over.

"Let me look."

I place his hand on the knobs, and he leans forward and puts his eye up to the eye piece. He moves the telescope away from the stars the scope was positioned on and hums as he turns the knobs.

"Ah, I see it."

I smile. "What?"

"The Cryin' Lizard. It's beautiful."

Sitting on the towel, I lie on my back. "Describe it to me."

"Well, it's the brightest star in the sky. It twinkles just for you. It's big, and there's no other stars by it. It really is the prettiest thing I've ever set eyes on, besides you." He leans away from the telescope and makes his way over to me.

"I'm sure it's amazing," I say, as he lays beside me.

He reaches his arm out, sliding his fingers into my hair. "Nothing could ever be as amazing as you. You've saved me when I needed you the most. You saved me from a life without love."

I kiss him. With all that I am, I give him everything. "No, Ryan, you saved me."

And I fell in love with my best friend, and we lived happily ever after.
The End

ACKNOWLEDGMENTS

Thank you for reading Save Me.

Did you know over 100,000 US service members have suffered eye injuries since 9/11- March 2013. Many resulting from brain injuries sustained from explosions or blasts?

Many soldiers, like Ryan, suffer from blindness after being sent home with brain injuries months after they return home.

The Miami Lighthouse for the Blind, established in 1931, is comprised of a diverse group of volunteers, who provide programs and offer fundamental teaching to the visually impaired.

www.miamilighthouse.org

A percentage of the profits from Save Me will be donated to the center. If you would like to donate you can follow the link above to learn more.

I know I took a huge risk blinding a major character, but I wanted their story to be real and challenging.

Many US soldiers return home with many problems from serving overseas. I wanted to touch on some of the issues.

Also, it was tough writing from a blind pov. Trying my hardest not to put any visual cues. And, to do it without telling with all the other senses. Try it, it's tough.

OTHER TITLES BY LOGAN CHANCE

Like A Boss (Book 1)

Love A Boss (Book 2)

The Sex Me Novella Series:

Date Me

Study Me

Save Me

Break Me

New, Sexy Standalones

Playboy, an Amazon Top 100 bestseller

Heartbreaker

ABOUT THE AUTHOR

Logan Chance is an Amazon Best Selling Author with a quick wit and penchant for the simple things in life: Star Wars, music, and pretty girls. His works can be classified as Dramedies (Drama+Comedies), featuring a ton of laughs and many swoon worthy, heartfelt moments.

For insights into his writing, games, awesome giveaways, and exclusive bonus content, sign up for his newsletter: https://www.subscribepage.com/i5y5s9

Don't be shy, follow Logan on all platforms:

Facebook: www.facebook.com/Loganchanceauthor
Twitter: www.Twitter.com/loganchance85
Instagram: www.instagram.com/loganchance85

Logan Chance is releasing his FIRST Mafia Romance, TAKEN, January 26, 2018.
You can add it to your Goodreads TBR:
https://www.goodreads.com/book/show/36624434-taken
Read on for a quick sneak peek:

Taken Sneak Peek

TAKEN SNEAK PEEK

A MAFIA ROMANCE

Releasing January 26th, 2018

Prologue

Seventy-two steps until my life ends. Mendelssohn's Wedding March wafts from the strings of the tuxedoed orchestra serenading my death. The white satin bridal gown and veil clings to me like a shroud.

One.

Two.

Three. I count to calm my galloping heart.

Cold eyes at the end of the aisle lock with mine, daring me to run. The golden wings of the turtledove necklace hidden within the bouquet of lilies fisted in my hand, cut into my palm.

Four.

Five.

Six hundred attendees smile under the watchful eyes of the marble saints. Murmurs of "So beautiful," and "God bless," turn to wailing shrieks of horror as a shot rings out dancing across the crescendo of the wedding march.

God isn't here today. And the only wedding will be a red wedding.

∼

Chapter 1

Rhiannon

"Shh, you'll get us caught."

"No one's going to find us. Don't be such a baby, Rhi."

"I'm not a baby," my voice raises a little with denial.

I hate when he calls me a baby. I'm eight years old and can do a ton of things for myself. Like, daddy lets me ride my bike around the neighborhood all alone. Well, really until the end of the street, but still. Plus, grownups say I have a mature soul; whatever that means. It doesn't sound babyish, though.

"No talking until we get outside," he whispers. He's so bossy. But, he is a year older than me, so I guess, technically, he is in charge.

We duck out the French door in the kitchen, into the dark, trying our best not to make a sound.

This probably isn't a good idea. Rescue the princess is a game we play often but never at night. The moon plays peekaboo in the cloud-covered sky, and we slip like mist across the damp grass, hopefully without being seen by the guards who always watch the grounds.

If my father found us sneaking out, we'd probably be murdered. You think I'm exaggerating, but I'm not. I've heard the staff whispering when they think I'm not listening. Once, I asked my mother if he's a bad man, and she told me never to say it again. She said he protects us from the other bad people of the world. So, I guess he's good to us.

Well, good to me, anyways. He doesn't care much for Xavier. Mom says he only tolerates him because he's Hannah's son. She's our maid, tall with beautiful hair the color of chocolate, and one of the nicest women I've ever met. Sometimes, when she brushes my long brown hair, I pretend she's my mother.

Don't get me wrong, I love my mom, but she's always busy entertaining my dad's boring friends when she's not working at his office. She's never around, so Hannah is a stand in for me after school.

Sometimes, until bedtime. I don't mind; it's more time I get to play with Xavier. He's really my only friend, my best friend, since most of the girls at school won't talk to me. I'm not sure why they don't like me, and I don't care.

"This way," Xavier directs, leading me down the uneven cobblestone path that cuts through the backyard.

He grabs my hand when I hesitate, and like always, I feel as if nothing can harm me out here with him.

"We're almost there," he reassures, taking us away from the safety of the house, towards the towering woods.

"Maybe we shouldn't," I hedge. Unsure, I glance over my shoulder for a moment. A light flickers like a beacon calling me back, through an upstairs window.

"No turning back." Xavier's blue eyes glow with anticipation of all the things I'm afraid of as he tugs me along. He's the opposite of me: fearless. I want to be brave, but I've never been this far out in the woods before. A blanket of twigs snap beneath our sneakers as Xavier tightens his grip on my sweaty hand. Crickets chirp and things I don't want to think about rustle through the darkness.

A small cabin, in a clearing, comes into view, and he rushes up the rickety stairs, to the front door, dropping my hand somewhere along the way.

Spooky shadows lurk inside the windows, and I hang back a bit, my sneakers cemented to the earth. "What's in there?"

"Don't be a fraidy cat."

"I'm not afraid." I raise my chin and step on the first wooden plank leading up to a small porch.

He opens the door. "Ready?"

I'm not, but I'll never let him know it, so I continue on and follow him into the unknown.

He flicks his flashlight on and scans the room. The dark walls are bare. One lone chair sits like a throne in the middle of the room with steel handcuffs attached to both arms.

"What is this place?"

"I don't know," he answers, looking over at me. "I followed your dad and his friends the other day down here."

"Xavier, we shouldn't be here. I don't think good things happen in this place. I don't like it here."

He grabs my arm, his blue eyes holding mine. "One day, I'll take you away from your father and all the bad things."

Xavier has never liked daddy either. His cold hard stare. The gruff in his voice when he yells at him for everything.

My father calls him a ...nuisance.

"What if I don't want to leave?"

"What could you possibly like about living with your father?"

I don't get to answer because there's a snap of a tree branch outside.

"Hide," he says, flicking his flashlight off. We crouch by the far wall of the small cabin, behind a table full of tools I don't understand.

The front door flies open. "Who's in here?" The sound of my father's voice startles us both. Xavier, eyes loaded with fear, slaps a hand over my mouth before I can answer.

Tucking my knees to my chest, I try to make myself invisible, and for a moment, I wish I was. My father will probably spank me for being out here, maybe ground me forever from playing outside, but it's nothing compared to what he'll do to Xavier.

He might even go so far as to fire his mother.

When my father shines his light around the room, we shrink back into the small alcove of the side. It's no use. Footsteps fall faster to our hiding spot and Xavier is yanked up by his hoodie.

"You're hiding like a rat," my father bites out. "Why are you in here?"

Xavier's eyes meet mine, and he gives a little shake of his head, warning me to stay silent. "Answer me," he yells so loud it feels like the walls vibrate.

"I was just exploring," Xavier finally responds.

"Exploring?" My father drags him to the chair and drops him down in it. "Come out of there, Rhiannon," he orders.

Reluctantly, I stand from my hiding spot. He flips on the light, and I squint against the fluorescent glare. He's scary when he's angry. Pinched face, flaring nostrils. And right now, he's madder than I've ever seen him. Hannah says to count when I'm afraid or upset and when I'm finished, it won't seem so bad. So, I count the steps in my head over to him to calm myself.

One.

Two.

Three.

I don't want to be a baby, but the tears start falling.

Four.

Five.

He grips my arm and yanks me in front of Xavier. "What are you doing here, Rhiannon?"

Through my tears, I answer. "I'm only eight, you can't expect me to make good choices."

He pulls his leather belt free from the loops, and then, he whips me. Over and over.

"Stop," Xavier yells. "It's not her fault. Punish me."

"This is your punishment, Xavier," my father shouts.

I count in my head, but the numbers jumble together; it hurts too bad. Finally, after a few more minutes, the hits cease, but the sting and burn continues. Uncontrollable shudders rack my frame, and the sound of my sniffles fill the space. I'm sure Xavier really thinks I'm a baby now.

My father leans down, an inch from Xavier's stricken face, bracing his hands on the arms of the chair. "Remember this lesson."

Xavier doesn't look at me on the entire walk back. My father strides ahead of us across the lawn and when he's out of ear shot, Xavier takes my hand.

"One day, Rhiannon, I will take you away from him."

I don't say a word. The look in his eyes tells me he isn't kidding.

Made in the USA
Monee, IL
11 July 2021